A heart-warming post-war family saga

Gentleman Jim

A heart-warming post-war family saga

Gentleman Jim

Penny Holmes

Published in paperback in 2021 by Sixth Element Publishing
on behalf of Penny Holmes

by Sixth Element Publishing
Arthur Robinson House
13-14 The Green
Billingham TS23 1EU
www.6epublishing.net

ISBN 978-1-914170-15-7

British Library Cataloguing in Publication Data. A catalogue record for this
book is available from the British Library.

Printed in Great Britain.

*I dedicate this book primarily to my mother
who had so many tales to tell on many occasions,
a woman who laughed a lot and always said
she could write a book of it all.*

*Also to my husband,
who has encouraged me
at every stage to finish this book
and has never failed to support me.*

Chapter 1

First one out is the best dressed. These words echoed in Lizzie's mind as she looked up at the high ceiling of the bedroom she once shared with her seven sisters. She lay on the counterpane of the iron-framed bed, her hand resting on the plain white envelope, and could almost hear her Mam's voice shouting up the stairs at them, "Be quiet, your Dad has to get up for work in the morning." She couldn't believe she had gone full circle back to this room.

The room was the largest of the three bedrooms, which accommodated another large bed in the corner. The carved oak headboard stood behind a huge soft mattress, which the girls argued about, over whose turn it was to sleep in it.

Just at the side of the bed was a large oak wardrobe, which held all the girls' clothes. Hannah, the eldest sister, always tried to get out first to get the pick of them. Years later, Hannah made a joke to everyone how the first one out was the best dressed. You never could keep an eye on everything with eight girls around.

The second room was Mam and Dad's. The room was large and airy with a dressing table taking its position in front of a large, narrow, paned glass window. The girls would often sneak in to put any make-up on, but trouble lay ahead if their mother saw any loose powder on her dressing table. The glass candlesticks were cleaned every day, and the brush and comb set, with silver on the back of them, never showed any signs of wear. It was Mam's pride and joy, left to her by old Auntie Edith.

The bedroom at the back of the terraced house belonged to the only brother, George. He couldn't wait to join the army and get away from his sisters and their silly idle chatter about nothing. They laughed at nothing and really got on his nerves.

Lizzie had grown up in a mining community of South Shields during the war years. Gerald Street and Arnold Street, with a hundred miner's terraced houses, stood alone in two long lines, backing onto each other by a back lane. Green grass and cornfields surrounded the area. There were two farms nearby where you could work doing some potato picking and make a bit of money, not to mention getting to know any new faces that might be working there that day.

Gerald Street overlooked the 'The Green Hut', which was the local school. Lizzie recalled her playmates that went without shoes when their fathers had no work and life was basic. At weekends, anyone in need went along to the police station in the town to see if they could get a pair of police boots to fit them. They were handed in when the Bobbies were issued with new ones. Lizzie always felt privileged that her Dad had a good job at the pit and they never went without good food, clothing and a fire to keep them warm.

Lizzie could almost hear the chatter of the back lanes all those years ago where they played for hours at hopscotch, marbles, tiggy and hide and seek. They called the lanes the top, middle and bottom corner. Friends spent time together with those of a similar age. The older crowd always made for the bottom corner where you could do your courting without being bothered by the younger children playing their noisy games.

But it was the year the war ended, when she finally left school and got her first job that her life really changed.

Lizzie closed her eyes and remembered.

Chapter 2

It was 5am and the Thompson household was stirring to the sounds of their mother coughing. Mam smoked too much and every day she woke up reaching for her Senior Service from the bedside table. She always nudged their Dad as she got out of bed. His usual grunt was her signal to carry on downstairs and put the pan of porridge on the kitchen range, where the small fire was kept burning night and day. There was always plenty of coal while Dad worked at the mines. Mam filled the large black kettle with water and placed it on the stove to boil up for tea. She then carried on into the front room to set the fire. Mam always cleared the ashes out at night so it didn't take long to get going in the morning.

Lizzie felt excited by the thoughts of the day ahead of her. She'd been unable to sleep during the night. It was to be her first day at work! She'd only just left school on Friday and now she was a working girl. She was to work in Moores Stores after her sister, Alice, had spoken for her. Alice had already proved what a good worker she was and was delighted when told her sister could have a chance of working in the shop.

Lizzie decided to get up; she knew her Dad would be in the lavvy all of twenty minutes, having taken his

Epsom salts. She was hoping to get a chance to talk to Mam before the others got up. She slowly crept out of bed so as not to wake Alice lying next to her; she slipped on her clothes and carefully picked up her pressed overall for work. With one turning glance around the room, she tiptoed out, down the steep stairs to join her mother. She almost tripped halfway down on a loose bit of carpet. Without thinking, she turned, placed her overall carefully on the stair above and began to straighten the carpet, pushing it up into the stair-rod. The paintwork could do with a wash, she thought. She stood up, picking up her overall, giving it a quick flick with her hand to remove any dust.

She nodded to her mother as she passed her poking up the fire and carried on into the kitchen to wash her face and hands. The kitchen door was slightly ajar and she could smell the tobacco smoke coming from the lav, where her Dad was reading the paper.

"How long will he be, Mam? Need the lav meself." Lizzie peeped through the crack in the door of the front room and could see Mam with the back of her skirt pulled high, warming her legs against the fire.

"He shouldn't be long, hinny. He's due to leave soon. Help yourself to porridge."

Lizzie did as she was told and, as she turned, she saw the large frame of her father coming through the doorway. She nodded to him, and he nodded back to her whilst turning the kitchen chair sideways so he could sit to pull on his pit boots. Lizzie filled her bowl, watching her

Dad squeeze into his overcoat, hunching his shoulders almost up to his ears to feel comfortable while doing so. He then took his cap, straightened out the peak and, with two hands, pulled it well down on his head, until finally, he pulled the peak forward almost over his hairy eyebrows.

Men folk never had much to say, and as he picked up his bait, he was making his way through the back kitchen door, turning slightly to say he was off. She watched his back as he walked slowly down the yard, reached up and lifted the latch, and Lizzie could see the small army of pitmen passing down the lane for the early morning shift.

Mam joined her in the kitchen, pulling out a chair from the table and breathing a deep sigh. She always did relax once Dad was off to work. Lizzie went out into the yard to use the lav and when she returned, Mam had poured them both a cup of tea.

"Well, lass, you'll be looking forward to today... first day at work."

"Yes, Mam," said Lizzie as she sipped away at her hot tea.

She thought she had loads to say to her mother, but when she sat in front of her there was a comfortable silence. Life was about to change.

Lizzie was thoughtful for a few moments and then suddenly stated, "I'm looking forward to me pay. I'm heading straight for Frederick Street with my first provident ticket, to buy some clothes."

"Not before you pay your board money, missy," replied

her Mam, raising her eyebrow on one side. They both laughed.

"I know that, Mam!" she replied, smiling at her mother.

The family had been making their way in the world over the last few years, despite the dramas of the war. Hannah had married and had one daughter called Doreen. They had been lucky and had managed to get a miner's cottage in Harton Lane.

The fifth sister, Sadie, had met a lad from Coventry whilst she was working in the munitions factory. They started courting and within six months of meeting, he had asked if she would marry him and go and live in Coventry. She had a small wedding in the registry office and was only to return for brief visits, reassuring Mam each time that they were safe and that no German bombs would ever dare hit her house.

Dorothy was the quiet one who worked in the General Hospital, as a domestic. Peggy and Sissie were in service in Newcastle, so you only got to see them on their day off. Gracie was the youngest and she was to start work at the hospital at Easter when she left school. Dorothy had spoken for her. Mam was pleased her family were making its way. Even George had flown the nest and was enjoying life in the army.

The household was coming to life now. Dorothy was all set to leave for the hospital. She never had much to say and was always busy with something in her hands. You felt you would interrupt something special in her thoughts if you disturbed her, so no one did. She did have a fella; Lizzie knew because one day she'd followed her down the yard and peeped into the lane to see her fall into someone's arms. They looked as if they would fall over if the other moved away. She watched them kiss so passionately, she thought for a moment it was another girl in the darkness. Not her sister Dorothy, not quiet Dorothy who never said boo to a goose.

Dorothy wouldn't eat in the mornings, something Mam didn't approve of. Dorothy was always ready to leave when she came downstairs. She picked up her coat out of the closet, quickly shuffling into it. She never looked around, only to pick up her checked headscarf, which she carefully unfolded, lay one corner down to line up in between her knees, bent slightly forward, and folded over the other corner to make a triangle. This done, she quickly stood up, picking up each outward corner and flicking it up above and over her head to fasten tightly under her chin.

"I'm off," she called, picking up her woolly black gloves and carrier bag containing her overall and sandwiches for her dinner break. Mam made sure she had that inside her.

Mam and Lizzie gave each other a glance and with that Mam said, "Watch what you're doing, hinny," and she watched as this quiet daughter left for a hard day's work, scrubbing floors on her hands and knees at the local hospital.

Alice was in the back kitchen now, helping herself to porridge. She looked over to Lizzie still sitting at the table, miles away in thought. "Our Lizzie, you better not show me up today. I don't want to get the sack because I spoke for you! And you better do as you're told. You know Mrs Butterworth won't take any cheek, so I've told you!"

Lizzie looked at Alice with that stubborn squint in her eye. "Shut your mouth, our Alice, I know what I'm doing."

Lizzie didn't, of course. She was really feeling nervous and could feel butterflies in her stomach. She'd only met Mrs Butterworth once and that was a frightening experience. She could hardly speak for the throbbing feeling in her neck. At the same time, colour was flushing over her, she could feel her face swelling with her eyes bulging forward in their sockets; at one point, she thought tears would flow out. Thank God, they didn't, she thought. She would just do her best, keep quiet and get on with whatever Mrs Butterworth told her to do.

Alice quickly finished her porridge. "Come on, our kid, you don't want to be late on your first day."

The girls got their coats and scarves on. Mam handed them their carrier bags with their bait in. She gave a loving smile to them both, and as they were leaving through the back door, she patted them in turn on their backs. "Now get on with you both and put your backs into your work."

The girls both smiled and left with Mam putting the latch on the backdoor.

With all the commotion suddenly gone, Mam gave herself a jolt as she remembered Gracie was still in bed. It wouldn't be long before she'd be leaving school. How the girl would ever get herself up for work, doing the shifts at the hospital, Mam couldn't imagine. She began shaking her head from side to side as she thought about it. She stood at the bottom of the stairs and shouted up, "Our Gracie, come on!" She paused for a second. "Time for school, you can't be late." She heard Gracie's usual groan and turned away now knowing that Gracie would get up.

That all done, Mam sat on the armchair in front of the fire. She put her hand inside the pocket of her pinny and took out her fags. Even the thought of the rolled tobacco in white paper made her feel relaxed. She popped the cigarette into her mouth, reached to tear off a piece of paper from last night's Gazette at the side of the fireplace, and lit it from the blazing fire. As she did so, her head tilted slightly backwards while she inhaled the smoke and relaxed back into the chair. There were no thoughts in Mam's mind but that Gracie would be off to school in ten minutes and then her chores would begin.

Chapter 3

Lizzie and Alice walked along the old mine railway track which led towards Boldon Lane, meeting up with a group of girls making their way to work. Alice knew most of them and kept on introducing her sister as they walked. As soon as they had passed, Alice proudly told Lizzie which shop each of them worked in and then under her breath she whispered little bits of gossip she knew would tantalise her wide-eyed sister.

The time passed quickly and before they knew it they had arrived at the far corner of Boldon Lane and the corner shop called Moores Stores.

Annie Parker was reaching up with the long pole to pull the shutters down. She was always in first, eager to please Mrs Butterworth.

"Hello, Alice. Is this your sister?"

"Yes, this is our Lizzie."

"Hello, Lizzie," was the cheerful reply.

Lizzie smiled and returned the greeting. She was feeling nervous now as she followed Alice into the shop. It felt so strange to her walking on behind the counter into the back shop.

"Hang your coat up over there, our kid," Alice said, "and hurry up."

Mrs Butterworth was already coming through the doorway. "Glad to see you girls got here in plenty of time. I like to see the shop sorted before the customers come in. Alice, you can get a bucket and mop and give the floors a going over. Lizzie, we'll see what you're like at cleaning windows. I want no streaks in them so you'll have to get your back into it. Come on, lass, I'll show you where everything is, your sister's got her own work to do."

Lizzie followed Mrs Butterworth. She was careful not to trip over anything as she carefully followed her boss's footsteps. She felt so awkward and clumsy but wanted to make a good impression on her first day. Mrs Butterworth pointed to the sink where the buckets and cloths were kept.

"You'll find all you need under there, lass. There's a new wash leather in the drawer." She glanced around at Lizzie who had a bird-like look in her eye, just as if she was waiting to be pounced on. "Come on, lass, we haven't got time for daydreaming." Mrs Butterworth went to the doorway, her head turning slightly as she spoke to Lizzie, but her eyes were looking out into the shop to see what the girls were doing. Mrs Butterworth had no time for young girls settling in. They just had to prove they were workers and they kept their jobs.

Lizzie bent down to find a bucket under the huge cupboard. She picked out a tin one, which she thought suitable. Just at the side, there were neatly folded cloths and a bottle of vinegar. She poured some of the vinegar into the bucket and then began to fill it up with water, stirring it with her hand as she did so. She then opened the drawer to pick out a new wash leather and get on with her work.

The bucket was heavy with all the water, but she was a strong girl like all her sisters and managed it easily. Lizzie was a tall, well-built, athletic-looking girl with strong shoulders, a large bust and small hips. Although she had poor, fine, black hair, this was more than made up for with a strong bone structure framing a pretty face with peaches and cream coloured skin.

As she walked through the shop, she knew all eyes were on her. They were wondering whether she would spill any on the floor, giving Mrs B the opportunity to bellow that she didn't want the smell of vinegar on her clean floors.

Lizzie kept her eyes straight ahead, leaning slightly to one side to balance the weight of the bucket and water. She was determined not to spill a drop until she got outside but the bucket seemed to have a mind of its own and swished the water from side to side until all the side of her legs were splashed. Lizzie wasn't bothered. Somehow outside the shop she could breathe easily again.

Suddenly, right behind her, was Mrs B.

Lizzie turned and couldn't help taking a deep, short, sharp breath. What now? she thought.

"Before you start, young lady, you'll need the steps to reach up to the top. Now go back through the shop and get the ladders from the back yard," said Mrs B, taking full advantage of her authority.

Lizzie could have kicked herself. Why didn't she think

about the ladders first before Mrs B had the chance to get on her back? It won't happen again, she thought to herself and that stubborn look came over her face once more.

She walked back through the shop. Alice glanced quickly at her but carried on as if too busy to be concerned. Of course Lizzie was too embarrassed. She'd just wanted to feel grown up and important but today was not to be one of those times.

She saw the ladders at the bottom of the yard, Mrs B again behind her.

"Lizzie," she shouted, "open the back yard door and take the ladders around the lane. The customers are starting to come into the shop and I don't want you knocking into anyone."

She glanced back with a half-hearted smile. "Alright."

At that Mrs B gave a quick nod of her head and, as she turned, she wondered if she would ever get these young girls into shape – it wasn't like this when she was a young lass.

Lizzie drew back the bolts on the door; she didn't have to stretch too far for the top one. She picked up the ladders and carried them under the doorframe of the back yard wall.

Once through, she tucked them under her arm and carried them around the corner to the side of the shop. For the first time, she looked across the road to the building of Wright's biscuit factory. She was taken aback by the noise of the lads who worked there, loading the tins of biscuits. She paused for a moment, catching the eye of a young man who was ticking off the stock while making notes on a clipboard. He eyed her up and down, but at the same time kept his head in motion with the tins being carried past.

Lizzie turned quickly, carefully placing the top of the ladder up above the window frame so she could reach the window. She wanted to act as if she had not taken much notice of this young handsome, dark haired lad, but as she looked in the glass she could see he was staring right across the road at her. The tins of biscuits had stopped going past him.

She quickly bent over, placing the wash leather into the bucket of water and wringing it out. As she climbed the ladder, she kept her eye on the reflection in the window... he was still watching. This time she got annoyed and glanced back at him.

"Had a good look, have you?" She regretted saying that as soon as it came out of her mouth, but she never could keep her mouth shut.

"Yes, I have," came back the reply. "Just started, have you? Haven't seen you before."

She ignored his comments and carried on with her job of cleaning the windows.

After a minute she looked through the glass and he had gone. She felt disappointed... he was really handsome.

The time passed quickly and before she knew it she'd been right around the whole shop, side and front. She caught Mrs B's eye, and accepted the half-hearted smile and a slight nod of her head like the one she had been given earlier that morning.

She must be pleased with me, Lizzie thought, otherwise I'd soon know about it. She bent down to the final corner of the window and polished off the damp patch, stepping back and tilting her head up towards the window top to admire her work.

"I'm glad the sun has gone in, no streaks showing!" she said out loud without thinking, then quickly picked up the ladders and started walking towards the back lane. She didn't want anyone to see her admiring her work, so she made a determined effort not to look back at the shining windows.

As she turned the corner into the back lane, she just had to look over to the factory to see if that handsome lad was in the yard but there was no sign of him. Never mind, she thought, there's always tomorrow... he must come out every day, otherwise how would he know she was new?

Before she went inside, she tidied up the yard. She was used to that. Everyone had a job to do at home and you never expected anyone to pick up after you. Once done, she made her way back into the shop where Mrs B was waiting for her.

"Good work, Lizzie, you're just like your sister and I can rely on my girls to clear up. It's time for a cuppa now, so you get the kettle on for the girls. We'll take it in turns for our breaks."

The day was over really quickly. Lizzie never served anyone in the shop; it seemed her job was cleaning today. She did more cleaning in the shop than she done at home for a week.

"Come on, our Lizzie," a voice called, "get your coat. It's time for home."

Lizzie looked around at Alice who was fastening the buttons of her three-quarter length brown jacket, turning as she did so and making it swing out slightly due to the skirt-like shape. Without saying a word, Lizzie left the cloth on the bench she was wiping and quickly made her way to the pegs holding all the girls' coats.

"Come on," she whispered to Alice. She was starving and wanted to be home for dinner. They knew their mother would have the table set and could almost smell the hot food that would be waiting.

Monday was washday, so it would be pea soup. Mam always made that so she could get on with the week's washing. Rain, hail, sun or snow, washing was done on Mondays in the washhouse in the yard. Lizzie was beginning to think it was better working in the shop than boiling up washing and scrubbing shirts with soap on the washboard. Mam would be at it all day. There was no wind today, so the house would be full of clothes drying off. The pulley line would be full and the clotheshorse would be around the fire, with steam filling the sitting room.

When the sun shone, the back lanes were filled with stretched lines of washing, as the woman in every household displayed her whites, freshly rinsed in Dolly Blue, the coloured clothes stretching from brick wall to brick wall.

The girls chatted on the way home. Alice had loads of gossip for Lizzie, who had no idea so much went on in the little seaside town of South Shields. She was beginning to wonder if all these tales were true. Anyway, she enjoyed the scandal so much that in no time they were outside their back door, smelling pea soup with potatoes and hearing their mother's voice telling them to get sat down before it got cold. Dad had waited tonight to have his dinner with the family. He'd had his bath in front of the fire before the girls got home. Mam would have scrubbed the coal dust from his back and he'd had time for a smoke and a nap in front of the coal fire. The familiar smell of drying clothes filled the air. It felt safe and homely.

The dining table stood behind the couch. Its drop leaves were raised so the family could sit around every night for dinner. The girls had lots to talk about to their Mam, while their Dad just sat quietly eating and slurping his tea from his saucer. The ritual was carried out so often no one took any notice of him pouring it from his mug onto the saucer… "Cools it down for me gums," he used to say. The only time it stayed in the mug was when he dunked a biscuit in it.

Dad sat at the top of the table. His dinner was always served first with his mug of tea. His newspaper rested in front of his plate, propped up by the milk jug. It was always best to wait until Dad had read his paper before you asked for the milk. Mam had decided early on as a mother to water the children after the meal when Dad had gone for his lie down upstairs. Once he was upstairs, he very rarely came back down, unless he was walking out for a pint down the road at the Golden Lion pub on Boldon Lane. This was rare during the week; he was usually too tired and fell asleep in bed for the night.

As Lizzie held an audience at the table, talking about her first day at the store and how she was kept so busy, no one noticed how quiet young Dorothy was, except for her Dad. He kept glancing over the top of his glasses while reading his paper. Although Dorothy never had much to say, he could see by her face that her mind was elsewhere.

Finally he got up, having finished his meal and reading the paper, but instead of going upstairs he sat on the armchair at the side of the fireplace. This caused a silence while the girls looked around at each other. After a pause, Mam stood up and said that she would be making a pot of tea. She never made a pudding on wash days, but there were always plenty of homemade biscuits. She turned slightly, glancing over at Dad, "Want another cuppa, hen?"

Dad shook his head and stared into the fire. He was going to wait to see what young Dorothy had to say for herself. Mam brought in the big pot filled with tea and Alice carried in a plate of biscuits. Gracie cleared up the plates and Dorothy carried out Dad's plate and mug with the salt and pepper pots. Then the girls all sat back down to resume their chatter. Dorothy was now aware her Dad had noticed how quiet she was, so she made a big effort to join in with her sisters which was something she rarely did and was usually happy to sit back to enjoy watching them.

When all the chat was exhausted, Mam gave a nodding motion with her head... the girls knew it was time to wash up. Everyone got on with this while Mam folded the checked gingham tablecloth, turned to the corner of the room to where the sideboard stood and placed the neatly folded cloth inside the draw. She glanced back at Dad, who was still looking into the fire, and she wondered what was on his mind.

While she dropped the sides of the table, she called out to the girls in the kitchen, "Bring in a bucket of coal."

She heard Dorothy say she'd get it so she carried on the chores to get her room back to normal for another day.

Dorothy went into the yard to the coalhouse. It was getting dark now and only the back kitchen light enabled her to see into the mountain of coal in the bunker. She filled the bucket full and as she did her thoughts wandered... she would have to tell them tonight.

She struggled past the girls in the kitchen, trying not to catch anyone with the coal dust from the bucket. The girls instinctively moved to one side to let her pass. Mam shouted over to Dorothy to leave the bucket and said Dad would put a few coals on the fire when he was ready and she'd use the rest in the morning.

"Come and give me a hand to turn the table back around," she added.

Dorothy slowly walked to her mother, who was now

noticing she was more quiet than usual. They turned the table and pushed it back up against the wall, two chairs were placed at either side while the other four were placed around the room.

Mam looked Dorothy in the face and asked, "What's up with you, my girl?"

Dorothy paused. No point in putting it off any longer, she thought, and replied she needed to talk to her and Dad when everyone had gone out.

A silence fell in the kitchen as the others heard what she'd just said. They started chattering again as if they were taking no notice, but in a large household you always know what's happening with everyone. The girls finished washing up and asked their mother if she had any other jobs for them. Mam told them they could go out now, and without another word the girls went back into the sitting room and began collecting their coats from the cupboard under the stairs.

They left and shut the back door behind them, pausing in the yard for a moment. Alice and Lizzie looked at each other but Gracie carried on into the lane. She could hear her friends' laughter while they played hide and seek and chased the boys. Alice and Lizzie started walking up to the top corner; usually they were interested in who was hanging out. But tonight was different.

Back home, Mam sat on the armchair at the opposite side of the fire to Dad. Dorothy looked at the couch, which was placed neatly in the middle. This is it, she thought, there's no going back, and before she sat down, she said, "I'm pregnant. I think I'm pregnant."

Her Mam quickly jumped to her feet and slapped her smartly across the face. The shock was too much for her to speak.

Dorothy dropped her head and cried, "I'm sorry."

Dad got up now and, placing his hand on his daughter's shoulder, he told her to sit down. She did this and Mam did the same, but sitting bolt upright. Her daughter was pregnant and this was a disgrace, bringing shame on the family.

"I want some explanations, lass," Mam said, her voice stern and almost shaking with anger, "and most of all..." She took a deep breath to compose herself. "...I want to know what lad has done this."

Chapter 4

Alice and Lizzie walked much slower up the lane that night; they were both clearly worried about Dorothy.

"What do you think is up with our Dorothy?" asked Lizzie as she turned her puzzled face towards her sister.

Alice replied, "Did you notice how quiet she was at dinner? Something bad must have happened at work. Do you think she's got the sack?"

The girls decided to wait twenty minutes and then make tracks back home. They were certainly in no mood for talking to the lads tonight.

As they started walking back, a young man who Alice had never seen before was leaning up against the wall at the side of the next lane. He was very tall and lean with broad shoulders and as she looked up towards his strong jawline, she found it difficult to take her eyes away from the mass of thick black hair surrounding his charming features. He was alone and quietly puffing away at a cigarette. He looked quite relaxed with one leg resting over the shin of the other. He looked at the girls and gave a half-hearted smile, which Alice noticed immediately and quickly returned. Lizzie was still looking down at the cobblestones in the lane, unaware of the interest brewing between her sister and this stranger as they were crossing the short stretch of road.

Alice was still glancing back, unintentionally expressing her feelings to this young man.

"Who do you think that is?" Alice whispered to Lizzie.

"Who?" was the only reply from Lizzie. She could not see a soul around, now that they were in the middle lane.

"The lad, on the corner, smoking," answered Alice, her tone now sharp.

Lizzie turned her head immediately but there was no one in sight.

Alice got annoyed with her sister and said, "Oh, you always go around with your eyes shut."

The girls carried on walking the few steps further to the back gate of the yard. They both stopped, not being able to decide who should open the latch first or even if it was alright to go in. They had only just stepped into the yard when they heard the almighty row; this was not the time to go into the house. The girls sat on the back doorstep, trying to make out from the exchanged voices if Dorothy had lost her job. They could hear the final words of their mother telling Dorothy to get off to bed, she would be talking to her father and they would talk again tomorrow night when she gets in from work.

The girls lifted the latch on the door and quietly walked in, taking off their coats. Alice indicated to Lizzie she would take the coats through to hang up. Mam and Dad were gazing into the fire. The girls knew not to speak to them.

"We're off to bed and we don't want any supper," Alice said quietly.

Mam looked over to them and gave a short lift of her head. No one spoke so the girls went upstairs to get into their night clothes. They both decided they would wash in the morning, instinct telling them not to go back downstairs to use the sink.

Dorothy was in the oak bed, her head facing the wall. They could hear muffled tears under the blankets.

"Dorothy, what's happened?" Lizzie couldn't resist asking. "Have you lost your job?"

"No, I'm having a baby," was the sniffled reply in the darkness.

No one spoke or noticed Gracie curled up next to Dorothy, only the silence could now be heard.

The next day, life carried on as usual. It was only when the girls were walking to Boldon Lane that the events of last night were brought up and they discussed all the possible things that would be happening next to Dorothy. They imagined the wedding that would take place and wondered who the father could be.

When the girls arrived, Mrs Butterworth was ready and waiting with her list of jobs for Lizzie, which would no doubt keep her busy all day.

She wondered if she would ever be able to serve a customer. After all the girls had changed into their smart white overalls, Mrs Butterworth handed a large envelope to Lizzie. "Take this over to one of the lads at the factory gate. The postman has left it with our deliveries, the stupid bugger!"

Lizzie stared at the envelope, and wondered if she would see the lad who counted the biscuit tins again.

She came out of the shop, looking across into the yard through the factory gates. There he was! Her heart leapt up to her throat, causing her to take a deep breath. He noticed her immediately and started to swagger over towards her. He likes himself, she thought to herself, looks too big for his boots. But as they were within a foot of each other, Lizzie could not help feeling this was the most handsome lad she had ever seen in her life.

"Come on, what you got for me?" he said, looking directly into her eyes.

"Oh, it's a letter. It came to the shop by mistake and I was told I had to bring it over to the factory… will you see it gets to the office alright?" She handed him the letter and as she did she noticed her hand shaking.

"Yes, anything for a pretty face," was the reply.

This caused Lizzie to almost throw the letter into his open hand and she found herself replying abruptly, "Make sure you do, it might be important."

He only smiled at her in return as he took the letter, but as she turned to walk away, he could not resist adding, "And make sure it's you who brings over any more letters." He paused for a second and added, "Like I said, I like a pretty face."

Lizzie's neck moved slightly backwards. She could not think what to say back to him, even though she wanted to tell him not to be so cheeky. She was simply pleased he thought she was pretty. She turned, giving him a polite smile. He kept his eyes on her as she walked towards the gate and just as she was about to leave, he shouted over, "I'll be at the the Tick tonight if you like to dance."

Lizzie felt as if time had stopped, though she was still walking towards the shop. The Tick, she thought, that's the Majestic. Her Mam would kill her if she knew she wanted to go to the town to that dance hall. All her sisters had always gone to the Miners' Hall for a dance.

She decided she would talk to Alice about it on the way home.

The day passed quickly and as the girls were leaving, Lizzie decided to quiz Alice about the dance. "Alice, now I'm working, I want to go to a dance," she said. "I'm getting too old to walk up and down the lanes. Will you take me?"

Alice looked sideways at her sister, who did not return her stare as she carried on walking, looking straight ahead. Lizzie wanted to act as normal as possible and she knew if she looked at her sister, she would give the game away.

Alice thought for a moment and then gave her reply. "That's a great idea. I haven't danced for ages and I love it. We'll go to the Miners' Hall on Saturday."

Lizzie was quiet for a moment and then she decided she would have to look at her sister this time. "Alice, I was thinking of the Majestic."

Alice stopped and quickly turned to stand in front of her sister. "The Tick?" she said. "Don't be daft. Mam would never let you go into Shields until you're at least eighteen."

Alice started walking along the track again, confident that would be the end of it.

But Lizzie was not deterred and answered, "Oh, come on, our Alice, we don't have to tell Mam."

This time Alice turned to reply very firmly that she was having none of it... this was to be her sister's first dance and everyone went to the Miners' Hall.

Lizzie knew she did not have a leg to stand on and that she would have to settle for that. Anyway, she thought, it was not such a bad idea, because she could learn to dance and then by the time she met the lad from the factory, she would be an experienced dancer. Her mind wandered back to him, while Alice prattled on about Kitty Patterson's latest scandal and the tales from the shop customers. But although Lizzie appeared to be listening to her sister, her thoughts changed to the lad at the biscuit factory. He looked much older than any of the other lads she knew from the back lane and hoped that he was not courting, or worse than that, married. She wracked her brain to think how she could bump into him; he was obviously much more sophisticated than anyone she had ever met before.

When they reached home, the table was set and there was a large steak and kidney pie taking pride of place in the middle, with all the cooked vegetables grown and picked from Dad's allotment surrounding it. Today was one of Mam's baking days with the house filled with the smell of freshly baked bread, stotty cake, scones, sly cake and a couple of fruit pies. It would also be the day for a volunteer to take Granddad Thompson's food parcel, down to Winskell Road and collect his washing. The girls took their mother's home cooking down twice weekly with one day to collect his washing and the other to return it. Grandma Thompson had died years ago before the girls had a chance to know her. Granddad always kept them talking for much longer than they planned to stay, telling them old stories from the past. Sometimes he told the same one over a few times, but they never showed any impatience. Mam had said the words so many times that they would be old someday and that they would have to rely on their own families to care for them.

Everyone sat around the table in their usual places, but tonight there was none of the usual chatter. They all knew about Dorothy and hoped that their Mam and Dad would tell them what was going to happen next.

As they began to help themselves to the vegetables, Mam cut the pie and shared it out between her family. The steam filled the air as she cut open the pie, and you could feel your nostrils open to take in the smell of the meat and gravy. Mam was a wonderful cook who never measured any of the ingredients. She had her years of experience, limited money and the need to fill up the stomachs of a large family.

The girls tucked into the light suet pastry and slowly the talking started. Dad began reading his paper and Mam smiled as she felt a wave of contentment come over her as the family enjoyed her meal. It was not long before they finished and the rice pudding was being passed around to anyone who had room left to fill.

As the spoons were placed in the bowls, Mam began to speak. "Me and your Dad have something to tell you all." It was so silent that you could now hear a pin drop. "We wanted it to come from this table first and it is nothing to do with anyone else in the neighbourhood. It will be a fortnight's gossip for them and there it ends." Mam paused as she looked directly around the table at her girls. "Our Dorothy is pregnant." She stopped when she said these words and then looked around at them all to see if there was any reaction.

The girls just looked into their laps and made no effort to speak, apart from Gracie, who asked if Dorothy was getting married. Mam looked over to Dorothy, who had not taken her eyes off her mother for a moment.

"No," was the firm reply. "Dorothy will not be getting married and we will have no more talk of that." She carried on. "The rest of the family will be here for dinner on Sunday. So, we'll have no more talk about it. Dorothy will have her baby at home and be with her family."

Dorothy's eyes welled with tears; she knew she would have her family's support. At that moment she wanted to run upstairs and be alone to cry herself to sleep but when her sisters started talking about the knitting they would start, she decided to sit still and brave it out.

The mood quickly changed and the girls got up to clear the table, while Dad sat for a little while longer reading his paper. It was not too long before he stretched back into his seat, and told Mam that it was a nice drop of gravy and that he'd be off for a nap. Of course, everyone knew he was off to bed. Alice said she would take Granda Thompson's food parcel and collect his washing. Mam was going to pop across to Aunty Edith's for a cuppa so Lizzie decided she'd be having a good wash-down at the sink, while Gracie went out in the lane.

Alice picked up Mam's shopping basket and left through the back door to follow the pathway along the railway track. She had not walked very far when she noticed the tall stranger, who she had seen the other night smoking at middle lane corner. He was walking in the same direction along the pathway. As he caught up to Alice, he asked if she would mind him walking alongside her, as he'd been asked by his aunt to deliver a parcel to a friend in Stanhope Road. Alice was pleased to have some company, which would take her mind off Dorothy. He told her his name was Tommy Robson and he was staying with his old aunt. Alice knew exactly who it was.

"Is that Bella Robson?"

Tommy nodded.

"I know Bella. She used to let us in her house for toffee apples when we were bairns." Alice smiled as she recalled how kind Bella was. "It was really sad when she got sick. Mam and the other neighbours go in and help out when they can."

"Yes, I know, it's g-g-g-ood of th-th-em." Tommy was struggling with his speech now; she had not noticed his stammer at first and was surprised how difficult it was for him to get his words out. Alice did not try to speak for him. She waited until he had finished and began to warm to his kindness and the concern he had for his Aunt Bella. She was obviously dying and, as he was the last in the family, he'd had to come home from his work on the farms. He began to tell Alice that Bella was his mam's sister. They had moved to Yorkshire when he was very young, as his dad did not want him to work in the mines when he grew up. They had done farm work ever since.

"Will you be finding work up here?" Alice asked him. "What can you do?"

He seemed shy, but managed to tell Alice he was a very good handy man. He could paint, wallpaper, do good joinery work and had also worked as a labourer to a bricklayer. He said he was sure he could brick lay on his own and would be going down to the council to ask for work next week.

Alice smiled. He seemed a really nice lad, and with so much going for him she forgot about his speech problem.

Very soon the couple reached Winskell's corner and Alice indicated where Granda Thompson lived. Tommy touched Alice on her shoulder and said it was nice to meet her.

Alice smiled and, as he walked away, she shouted over, "If you want to make some friends, there's the dance in the Miners' Hall on Saturday. It's that building down there." Alice pointed nervously with her eyes over the road. "It starts at seven. You'll get to know the lads and you may even get to know someone from the council who might put in a good word for you."

A large smile came over Tommy's face. What a nice lass, he thought. He thanked her and said he would see her there.

Alice turned, feeling a spring in her step, then she realised with horror that she had invited him out. She hoped he did not think her too forward. She didn't know how she'd had the nerve to come out with it like that. Then she consoled herself... she must have felt sorry for him, after all he was a stranger and needed to make some friends.

Granda Thompson lived in a tiny ex-miner's cottage. Alice walked straight into the tiny hallway. "Yoo hoo," she called, "it's only me. How are you, Granda?"

The conversation took its usual course with him telling her about his arthritis and how he was stuck in that chair all day. He coughed and spluttered as he spoke; the mines had taken their toll on him. He started to raise his bent old body up from the chair, telling Alice as he did so that the kettle was boiled on the stove. Granda had been a tall well-built man but now Alice thought how small his body looked in his string vest, tucked into his baggy trousers, which were held up by a large, black, buckled leather belt, which he must have had since he was a young lad. It had so many cracks in it you could not imagine it staying together much longer. She watched him carefully as he stretched up to the mantelpiece for his tobacco to begin filling his pipe.

"What you waiting for, lass?" he said. "The kettle's boiled."

Alice muttered under her breath, followed by a smile, and carried on into the cold scullery to brew some tea. She thought to herself, it's going to be a long night... it was always a bad sign when he filled a new pipe.

Chapter 5

Lizzie's first week at work was over quickly. She was so happy when Friday came around and all the girls were given their wage packets from Mrs Butterworth. The girls, who were all single, discussed what they would be buying. Most of the girls made their own clothes. The market was always popular on a Saturday, for wool and material. There were always plenty of patterns available now that the war was over and people began to enjoy the fruits of their labours. However, that did not change the frugal attitudes they had been brought up on and everyone still liked a bargain.

The girls left the shop in buoyant mood and, as Lizzie and Alice walked home, they decided they would be buying some new material. If they worked together on the sewing machine, they could get two dresses made for the dance. Lizzie hated sewing, and knitting was definitely out of the question which was very unusual in their household. Alice looked sternly at Lizzie. If she wanted to get out to the dance, she had to do her bit.

The next morning, they got up early so they could catch the early trolley bus from Stanhope Road to the town. As soon as they got to the market, Lizzie got her eye on some pretty grey material with large red roses printed on it. The background had white lines shining through which made it very striking.

"I've seen mine," said Lizzie as she reached over to the roll of material.

Alice thought it looked a bit gaudy but decided not to say anything. "Good, that saves a bit time. I think I'll go for that blue material with the little yellow flower print."

The girls paid for their yards of material, which had been carefully worked out by Alice, so as not to have any waste. She told Lizzie she had allowed for the pattern and the bias. They now needed to go the next stall for the thread. The girls also decided on some ribbon for their hair, to match the dress material. They giggled as their plans came together.

Once done, they had to run for the trolley bus, which was just about to leave the market. It was always a bumpy ride, but somehow the noise and the folk making small talk brought a comfortable feeling of home to the girls. Soon they were walking up the lane towards their yard. Alice gave Lizzie her orders and told her that Mam would have the sewing machine set, ready in the corner of the room. Lizzie marched straight into the room and laid the material out flat on the floor so that she could overlay the pieces of the paper pattern carefully on top of the material.

The girls moved quickly once they got started. Mam asked for the thread so that she could fill the shuttle. Then the sisters and their mother got to work on the dresses.

No one spoke. The girls worked together to pin out, cut and tack, and it was not too long before Lizzie was able to try on the bodice of the dress.

"It's great," she said and then handed it over to her mother to sew.

Alice handed Lizzie the skirt and told her to tack it against the bodice. "What about the zip? We forgot to buy zips!"

Lizzie's stomach churned, but was quickly calmed again when Mam said she had a tin full in the sideboard, saved from all the old rags over the years.

"It's well seen you don't sew, our Lizzie." Mam smiled to herself. Lizzie and Gracie, her two youngest were so different from the rest. They did not knit, sew or even cook very well; she wondered how they would manage when they had their own homes and family to look after.

It took the rest of the day to finish both dresses. Lizzie wished she had waited and got a provi ticket; at least she could just have walked into the shop to buy one, without all this fuss. Still, she thought, it was nice of Alice to take so much trouble, and after all, Alice was doing all this to take her to her first dance.

All through the afternoon Dad had sat with his chair facing sideways to the radio, his head was pushed almost next to the speaker, listening to his football and the results for his pools coupon. Mam stopped every now and then to make him a mug of tea, a smile of pleasure on his face as it was handed to him on his lap.

As Mam helped the girls, she remembered how she had to make do and mend when she was a lass. Every old woollen jumper and cardigan was pulled out and re-knitted into a new one. The trick was to add a ball of different coloured wool, add a new stitch to your pattern and no one would know any different... you had a new garment. Mam only stopped helping the girls with the dressmaking to prepare dinner. She was cooking mince and tatie with dumplings tonight. She always looked forward to her Saturday out with Dad, when they went to the Golden Lion pub. She liked to get the dinner and washing-up over and done with as quickly as possible. Tonight would be a busy night; everyone would need to wash at the kitchen sink. However, Mam and Dad were always first, as they left the house at half past six every Saturday.

As the last pools score came in, Dad shook his head as he dreamt of what might have been. "Come on, lass," he said to Mam, "get ya glad rags on."

Mam just smiled. She was ready and putting her powder on, leaning over towards the mantle mirror. The finishing touch was a smudge of lipstick, with a final look down at her stockings to check the seams were straight. She was glad there was no more drawing lines up the centre of the back of her legs. That could never replace the feeling of real stockings next to your skin.

"Ready when you are," she called to him through the kitchen door.

Dad was just washing off the last bit of shaving soap

from his face. He stretched over to the chair where his clean white shirt hung alongside his newly pressed trousers. His best suit had been coming out every Saturday night for five years.

Mam came in with the clothes brush to brush him down. "There now," she said. "You look as good as new. That suit was a good buy."

He gazed at her, his head tilted showing frowns in his forehead. "You only bought me this to wear at Aunt Mary's funeral."

"Well," came the chirpy reply, "I didn't want you showing me up. You'd had that old grey one since before the war."

They smiled at each other now; they had laughed about this story since Mam came in with the bargain, for her man, all that time ago.

They called upstairs to the girls to let them know they were off. The giggles from upstairs, as the girls tried on the new dresses, made them both smile as they left the house. They were very proud of their family.

They walked down the old track towards Winskell's corner and strolled into the Golden Lion pub. Each week, old friends and familiar faces sat in the same seats. If anyone was later than usual, there was always someone who would speak up for your place. The gossip never changed, always family, grandchildren, aches and pains. Unless of course some new scandal came to light… this would always last two weeks or so. Mam thought of her daughter now, she would be the gossip in a few weeks time, when she began to show. But she put those thoughts behind her. She wanted to enjoy her stout and a singsong.

Back home the girls had started getting washed at the kitchen sink. They were so excited, they hardly noticed Dorothy coming in from her hospital shift. She looked the girls over and asked where they were going. As they began to tell her about their day, buying material and making dresses, Dorothy was looking into the oven to get out her warm dinner. As she sat down to enjoy it, the girls asked her if she wanted to come.

She smiled and said she was much too tired. "I just want to get my feet up," she added.

The girls felt a twinge of guilt, but the excitement soon took over again.

They slipped into their new dresses and straightened up their stockings just as their mother had earlier. Dorothy asked where Gracie was and the girls said she was with her pals in the lane. It would not be too long before she was in and Dorothy would at least have some company.

Lizzie looked in the mirror, admiring her curves as she turned her body sideways. She had a good figure with shapely legs. Her hair was too fine, she thought, as she pushed her hairgrips gently into place once again. She leaned forward into the mirror and pinched her cheeks and pouted her lips to check her lipstick. Lizzie had little need for make-up, her skin was flawless and she was gifted with excellent bone structure, although this never occurred to her at that age… she was far too busy with life.

As they made their way down the lane, she noticed how they were both almost skipping; the butterflies in her stomach were totally out of control and she could feel her cheeks glowing.

"Do I look all right?" she questioned Alice, watching her sister's face carefully for any signs she may not 'fit in'.

"You look great. Ya bound to get a lad tonight."

Lizzie smiled, but she didn't want a lad, she only wanted to get to know the one from the factory. This was a practice night before she got around to getting to the Majestic.

"Anyway," said Alice, "what about me? What about this dress? Can you see any threads hanging anywhere?"

Lizzie looked her sister up and down as they talked.

"It looks really nice, our Alice."

It was not too long before they reached Boldon Lane.

"Have you seen the queue?" said Alice.

Lizzie looked across the road to the crowd waiting outside.

"It looks as though the doors are opening now. I can't wait to get inside and see who's out." Alice began to wonder now, as she glanced through the sea of faces, if Tommy would be there. She had thought of nothing else since they walked to Winskell's corner on Wednesday.

She told Lizzie to hold onto their cardigans. "If we get a seat, we can leave them on the chairs and no one else will sit there. After we've done that, we'll get a drink of something. We'll need that for the end of the dances. I hope someone gets me up."

Lizzie looked at her sister. "I thought you were going to show me how to dance?"

Alice glanced back at her sister, "Don't worry, once the women start dancing together I will... but listen, if a fella asks you, just say yes and he'll lead you around. You'll soon get the hang of it."

Lizzie froze. She hadn't thought of anyone asking her to dance and was now wishing Alice had shown her a few steps in the house before they came.

Alice spotted a free table. "Quick over there, our Lizzie."

The girls dashed across the dance floor, almost falling into the seats in case they missed them.

"Oh, there's Kitty coming over," Alice whispered as she got settled. "Looks like she's on her own, our kid."

Kitty had no hesitation in walking up to their table. "Hello, Alice. Mind if I join you? My friend hasn't turned up and I was desperate to get out tonight. My mother's driving me mad."

The girls smiled at Kitty. She always had a reputation, but when you got to know her she was great fun to be with.

"Have you seen anyone you like yet?" Kitty was eyeing up the young men as she asked the question.

Alice answered first. "No, we've just got in and grabbed these seats. What about you?"

Kitty shook her head but her eyes were still following the lads around the room.

Lizzie looked at Kitty now. "What you like at dancing?" she asked.

Kitty now had her eye on someone and was very slow to reply. Eventually, not really answering the question, she said, "Might have me eye on someone now!"

Lizzie decided not to ask again and left Kitty to do her 'eyeing'. She was beginning to feel a little uncomfortable and asked Alice if she should get the drinks in. Alice gave her a nod and with that Lizzie got up to make her way to the queue for drinks. As she edged past people, she noticed someone looking in her direction; it was Billy Jackson from school. His smile beamed across the room and Lizzie felt obliged to return one. That was all the encouragement he needed and he began to walk over to her.

"Lizzie," he said in amazement, "how are you? Have you started working yet?"

"Yes," replied Lizzie but she did not look at him. Instead, she leaned out, tilting her head backwards and looking up the queue.

Billy carried on. "I heard you were going to Moores Stores. Did you start for them?"

"Yes," again Lizzie replied, hoping she would recognise someone in the queue so she could move away from him.

Billy continued, staring wide-eyed at Lizzie. "I've started for Swans. I'm an apprentice electrician. My dad spoke for me."

"Great," said Lizzie. She turned to Billy, realising she could not see anyone she could talk to, so Billy would get her attention. "What's it like then?" she asked.

"Aw, the lads are great but they play a few tricks on me. I'm getting used to it now and it should be good money when I'm out of me time."

Lizzie thought Billy did not look too bad after all.

"Can I dance with you when the band starts?" he said.

Lizzie froze for a moment, and then decided Billy was probably a good one to start her practice on. "Yes, okay, Billy. I'm sitting over there with our Alice. Come over when the music starts." Then she turned away.

Billy read her body language and he knew it was time to leave. He was not in the least bit offended, in fact he was quite pleased to get a dance with Lizzie Thompson.

Lizzie got drinks for herself and Alice. She had not thought to ask Kitty, but then she decided Kitty could get her own. As she approached the table, she noticed Kitty had left and was talking to a lad she recognised from Wright's biscuit factory. With a fleeting thought, she wondered if Kitty knew the lad who counted the biscuit tins… But then her thoughts were taken over by seeing that Alice was talking to a stranger. She seemed to know him, but how could she know someone that she had never seen before.

Lizzie stood perfectly still; she could not reach her seat because the stranger was leaning across the table, taking all her sister's attention. She coughed and in that moment the stranger turned and Alice looked up at her.

"I've got our drinks."

No one answered immediately and then Alice said, "I came with my sister. This is Lizzie. This is Tommy. He's Bella Robson's nephew."

As Alice finished her introductions, they both unconsciously looked each other up and down and then nodded. Tommy moved to one side so that Lizzie could slide into her seat. Alice pointed to the seat that Kitty had just left and told Tommy to sit down.

Lizzie stared at her sister now with disapproval; she did not want to be stuck with him all night. She began to wonder again how Alice got to know him.

Alice took the drink from her sister and was about to explain how she met Tommy, when the bandleader moved to the microphone and announced, "Take your partners for the first waltz."

Tommy looked at Alice. "Would you like to dance with me, Alice?"

She was clearly delighted, not noticing the glare that Lizzie was giving her as she took Tommy's hand and followed him.

Before Lizzie had time to think, Billy Jackson was standing at the table.

"You said you'd have the first dance with me, Lizzie."

She looked up at Billy's smiling face and lifted slowly from the chair. This is it, she thought, now I'll see if I can dance.

Everyone took their partners to the floor, jostling to create their own space as the floor filled for the first waltz. Billy took command of Lizzie and began to lead her around the dance floor. She was amazed how easy it was and how well Billy could glide her around… she felt like she was floating.

She looked directly into his eyes and said, "Where did you learn to dance, Billy?"

Billy felt a twinge of excitement again, just as he had when he noticed her across the room. "Oh, me mam taught me and my sister from when we were young. We didn't like it at first, but she made us copy all the steps off her and now I love it."

Lizzie nodded at him and smiled broadly. This was just what she needed before she went to the Majestic. She reckoned it would not take her long to learn with a good partner like Billy. What's more, she sensed he would be keen to help her.

Alice was really enjoying dancing with Tommy; they glided around the floor together as if they had been partners all their lives. Tommy felt so at ease with Alice that his stammer was in control as he felt her warm body near to him. This is the girl I'm going to marry, he thought to himself, she's everything l could wish for. Alice was deep in thought also. The dancing seemed to make her mind drift away and she too was looking into the future.

As the music stopped, they both took in a deep breath. Alice placed her hand on her chest. "I need a drink. Tommy, how about you?"

"Yes, okay. I've left mine at one of the tables. I'll just

go and get it. Would you like another one brought to your table. I hope you and your sister don't mind me joining you?"

Alice quickly glanced around, looking for Lizzie; she'd enjoyed dancing with Tommy so much she'd totally forgotten about her. "Oh, she won't mind, just come over." With that final remark she stood at the edge of the table, looking in every corner for her sister. As her eyes glanced around, she was surprised to see Lizzie was twirling around underneath Billy Jackson's arm. They were doing the Jive. Alice's mouth fell open. Billy could really dance and people were making room for them, they were so good at it.

"Well, I don't believe it," she said. "It's a good job I've met up with Tommy or I would have been on my own." The words flowed out of her mouth just as Tommy was joining her.

"What did you say, Alice?" he asked.

"Nothing..." She paused. "Just that my sister's got a partner, so we won't be seeing much of her tonight."

Tommy looked over to the dance floor and smiled to himself as he thought how good the couple looked together, as if they were made for each other...

Chapter 6

Neither girls wanted the night to end; it had been a great success. Finally, as Lizzie and Billy held hands and strolled over to the table to join Alice and Tommy, Billy asked Alice if he could walk part of the way home with them. He had already asked Lizzie but she was concerned about her sister and still wasn't sure about Tommy.

"Oh yes, you can," Alice said. "We can all walk up together. Tommy is staying with his aunt, over our back lane."

The girls strolled on ahead with their cardigans over their shoulders. The lads introduced themselves and Tommy began telling Billy how he would be looking for work.

"My uncle Ronnie is a builder," said Billy. "I'm sure if you're a good worker, he'll give you a start. He's working in the town at the moment. I tell you, since the war he's never looked back even with all the council work going on. I'll ask him if you like."

Tommy turned now, looking Billy directly in the eye. He knew his stammer would hold back his words when he was excited, but he managed, "Billy, I'd really appreciate that. I need to get settled here. With my aunt being so ill an' all, this would be a great start for me."

"Oh, that's settled then," Billy said. "You can show me

where your aunt lives and I'll call one night and let you know what's happening."

Tommy looked straight ahead now, taking a deep breath as he did so. He put his hands in his pockets and started glancing down thoughtfully as Billy carried on telling him about the shipyards.

The girls began walking along the road. It would be a long walk, but no one noticed. They linked arms as Alice began to tell Lizzie how she noticed Tommy at the corner of the lane one night when they were walking home. They laughed as Lizzie recalled the night and remembered how she had turned around but saw no one.

"Yes," said Alice, "that was him." She balanced herself on their linked arms as she leaned forward, tilting her head in front of her sister to savour her reaction. They laughed again. They forgot about the lads following them, but it was normal to walk with your girlfriends while the lads talked amongst themselves. This was until you almost reached the door, when you would indicate and let them know this was far enough.

Soon they were at the lane. The girls turned, with Lizzie automatically moving away from her sister to give her a private moment with Tommy. Tommy could feel his hands starting to sweat as he reached forward to hold Alice's tiny waist. Alice looked up into Tommy's eyes as she rested her hands over his wide chest. This was her perfect man, she thought.

"I've had a great night, Alice," he said. "I'm so pleased you were at the dance. I only went because I hoped you would be there." He wanted to tell her about the prospect of a job, but instead, he said, "Can I kiss you? I know we've only just met but…"

And with that remark Alice stretched up from her ankles and their lips met with a gentle passion they both controlled.

Billy had caught up to Lizzie now and gently took hold of her hand. He pulled her slightly so she had to turn and he caught hold of her other hand. With their arms outstretched, Lizzie kept quite still. She really didn't know what to make of Billy.

He then leaned forward and kissed her cheek. "Fancy coming out with me next week, Lizzie? I'd like to take you to the wrestling in Newcastle."

Lizzie's jaw dropped. She'd never been to Newcastle, let alone a wrestling match.

"A wrestling match?" she said, almost shouting and getting a, "Ssshh," from her sister.

Lizzie was staring at Billy now. "Have you been before?" The excitement was echoing in her voice.

"Yes, a while ago with me brother and his mates, but women go and I'd love to take you, Lizzie."

"Okay," was her reply.

Billy's eyebrows raised now as he quickly told Lizzie to meet him at South Shields train station next Saturday afternoon at 12.30pm. He was so excited, he kissed her on the cheek again, then moved away with a wave and said, "See you next week."

Lizzie stared at him as he walked down the lane. Billy was getting more interesting by the moment.

She turned now, looking at Alice and Tommy cuddling with no movement.

"Come on, Alice, I want to get to bed."

Tommy pulled away first and said, "You better go in with your sister. It would be nice to see you tomorrow. Why don't you call across to see my aunt?"

What a good idea, thought Alice to herself, then it would not be so obvious they were wanting to see each other.

"All right, Tommy," she said. "I'll come over after me Dad's cooked breakfast."

"Your dad?" said Tommy.

"Oh yes, he does it every Sunday morning so Mam can have her lie in."

Tommy smiled as he imagined the scene and said, "Well, any time you like. I'm not sure what time Aunt Bella gets up, but I'll be up early and waiting."

This brought a huge smile to her face and Tommy thought how beautiful she was.

They slowly pulled away from each other, Alice only turning away when their final fingertips parted. "See you tomorrow then…"

Tommy watched her open the latch on the back gate and then proceeded to walk down the lane to his aunt's house.

Lizzie was in the yard waiting for Alice. "Come on, I thought you'd never come in. Are you in love or something?"

The girls laughed, but Alice knew her sister had spoken the truth.

As they opened the door into the kitchen, Mam and Dad were sitting at the kitchen table having their fish and chips. Every week was the same… when they left the Golden Lion pub, they headed straight for the chip shop. This was another meeting place for gossip, although with all the drink inside everyone, it was difficult to make sense of the one line banter that passed back and forth.

Mam smiled at her daughters. "Had a good night, lasses?" she asked as she watched their beaming faces.

The girl's replies were in chorus with each other. "Great, Mam, can I pinch a chip?" The girls leaned over and helped themselves to a couple of chips, and then they carried on through the sitting room upstairs to bed. They did not respond to their mother asking if they wanted any supper. They must have had a good night, she commented to her husband. All was silent, Dorothy and Gracie asleep as the sisters changed into their nightdresses for bed. The girl's spoke no more to each other, their evening thoughts keeping their minds occupied.

Sunday was a family day, but this was also Mam's morning to have breakfast brought up to her in bed. Dad was always up early to get down to his allotment. His first job on his way out was to go into the fields and collect wild mushrooms to cook with the bacon and eggs. Then, with an armful, he would carry on his walk to tend to his garden and bring home fresh vegetables for the Sunday dinner. The allotment was a special place for working men; it was their space, where they could exchange a few words with no meaning, just acknowledgement that they were amongst friends.

The allotment fed the whole family with fresh produce all year around. The only items Mam shopped for were groceries, which the girls brought home from the store. Meat was bought on market day, when she would get a butcher's wrap containing a nice big joint for the dinner and usually some bacon, sausage mince and some lap or neck end chops. Mam always managed to get a sheep's head for broth or a ham shank for Mondays (washday) dinner. On Sunday afternoon, when dinner was finished, she would start baking bread, savoury mince pie, fruit pie and scones for the tea. Sometimes this would help out for a couple of days, but usually Mam would be baking twice a week.

Dad returned home with the parcel of vegetables which he laid out on the kitchen bench. As the girls began to get up, they joined him in the kitchen and began to prepare the dinner. Alice scraped at the dripping bowl to spread over the meat tin and added that to the fat covering the meat. She took it into the sitting room where the fire was blazing to heat up the range oven. The smell coming from the back kitchen, where Dad was cooking the breakfast was making everyone's mouth water. He had already dished out the sizzling bacon and mushroom and you could hear the crackling of the eggs cooking in the pan.

"Help yourselves to the fried bread, hinnies," he called out. "There's plenty done. And get your mother's clean knickers off the mantel with the rest of her stuff and take them up for her. Here, Lizzie get this plate up to her afore she starts shouting for it."

Lizzie picked up the hot plate with the cloth next to the oven and made her way up the stairs. She followed behind Gracie's footsteps as her sister took up their mother's underclothes so she could warm them under the covers before she dressed.

On Sundays, all the Thompson family would visit Mam and Dad's. The house would come alive with the gossip from Peggy and Sissie, who came on their day off in service from Newcastle. The family would hear how the big houses were decorated and what the ladies wore were especially when they went to the theatre. Gracie always thought they were talking of another world. She found it very hard to imagine going downstairs into a huge kitchen with meat hooks hanging and knives of every size and shape. She thought it sounded like a torture chamber, just as the ones she used to see on the Saturday morning matinee. However, she liked the idea of being waited on hand and foot.

Hannah and her husband Geordie would bring their two year old daughter Doreen. Every Sunday she was spoilt by all the girls fussing over her. No one could resist her whims and gave her whatever she pointed at. Only Hannah showed disapproval. She said she had a right job getting her to bed on the night time, because she thought she should still be getting her own way. Children must have a bedtime.

"I don't want a spoilt brat," Hannah would say. But she always followed her statements with a smile. Doreen was the first grandchild for the Thompsons and everyone adored her.

The house began to buzz with noise as everyone arrived. Dad's radio was echoing Family Favourites in the background, and Mam was making her way through the sitting room into the kitchen. The sisters had all taken their places, preparing the vegetables. This brought a smile to Mam's face as she lifted her shoulders and sniffed the smell of the meat cooking. Nothing burning, she thought to herself. She started filling the large tin pans with water and scattering small handfuls of salt over them. Mam turned her head now towards the girls.

"Alice, have you put the rice pudding in the oven?"

"Yes, Mam, it's in," she said and carried on with the gossip.

Alice was beginning to think of Tommy now and wondering if she could get out before dinner.

"Mam," she said, "I've promised to pop over and see Bella Robson. Should I go over now before the dinner's ready?"

Mam thought it was a nice thought and saw motive in Alice's gesture. "Yes, hen. It'll be ready about half past twelve."

"Thanks, Mam," said Alice and she slipped out the back kitchen door with no one noticing.

There was a spring in her step as she made her way down the lane. She heard the latch open on Bella's back door and as she was about to walk in, Tommy opened it.

"Oh Alice, I was just thinking about you and came to see if you were coming down the lane."

"That's funny," said Alice, "us thinking of each other at the same time!"

She followed Tommy into the small familiar yard and watched his broad frame open the back door. When they got inside, Bella was busy with her hooky mat. She had rolled balls of cut out strips of material, which came from her dead husband's old coats and trousers. These were laid neatly out at her side. The oblong frame of sacking cloth was stretched out and she was weaving the material with in and out movements.

Alice smiled at her. "Hello, Mrs Robson," she said. "You never stop, do you?"

Bella Robson turned to her stiffly, very slightly. The arthritis in her body made it difficult for her move. "Yes, hinney," she replied. "I'm getting on with it. No use grumbling about old age, that's all it is."

Tommy and Alice looked at each other. They wanted to be alone in the sitting room but Alice had come to see Mrs Robson and it would look bad if they ignored her.

Bella sensed the young ones' thoughts and said,

"Why don't you two go for a little walk across the fields. I bet you've got an hour afore your dinner's ready, Alice."

Alice looked at Tommy and he took the lead. "Come on, Alice. It's a lovely day. I could do with some fresh air."

With that they moved past Bella and made their way out. Bella Robson was a good woman who did not expect help from anyone. She was happy Tommy had found a friend.

Tommy took hold of Alice's hand as they made their way over the fields. Alice turned her head to look back; she did not want anyone to see her holding Tommy's hand in case the gossip started. She wanted to introduce him to her Mam and Dad first.

The sun shone down as they walked and they began unconsciously swinging their arms and almost skipping.

"Let's sit down here for a while, Alice. I'd like to talk to you."

Alice looked questionably at Tommy. He looked very thoughtful and she sensed he was going to talk very seriously.

"Look, Alice," he said. "I know this is very sudden and I have to say I never thought this would happen to me, I mean, you hear about it happening to other people, but I never..."

Alice stopped him and said, "What are you trying to say, Tommy?"

"Alice..." Tommy began to stutter badly now. He really

wanted this to go well, with a nice poetic sentence. He would just have to settle for less and spilled out, "I'm in love with you, I knnnooow t'ssss silllly to you."

Alice took his hand. She felt his discomfort and warmed to him even more. "I feel the same," she said and with that they moved together to kiss.

Back home, dinner was coming together and the girls were setting the table. Lizzie suddenly realised Alice was not in the house.

"Where's our Alice, Mam?"

"She's over seeing Bella," was Mam's reply.

Lizzie's voice was disgruntled. "Got out of helping with the dinner."

Mam was annoyed now. "It would do you well to be a bit more charitable, our Lizzie. That woman's not well and could do with a bit of company."

Lizzie started to mutter under her breath as she swung out the best white Sunday tablecloth. "Seeing Tommy Robson, more like."

Mam turned to Lizzie. "What did you say?"

"Nothing," was the quiet reply, but Mam was too busy to make an issue of it.

As Alice and Tommy came back up the lane, Alice turned to Tommy and said, "I'd like you to meet me Mam and Dad. Why don't you come over this after and you can have ya tea with us?"

Tommy was delighted but was careful not to be

presumptuous. "Well, if you're sure that's alright, Alice. I know you said you have everyone over on a Sunday. Will your Mam not have enough on her plate?"

Alice smiled, looking into Tommy's big brown eyes. "Of course not, the more the merrier."

Tommy smiled too, thinking how lucky he was. "Well, I won't kiss you, Alice, in case any of the neighbours are watching. What time should I come over?"

Alice pulled away from Tommy and as she did she lifted her hand in a wave. "See you about half past four."

Tommy nodded as he turned to go into his aunt's yard.

When Alice reached home, everyone was just about to sit down.

"Come on, Alice," said Mam, "sit yourself down. We're just about to start. How's Bella?"

Alice made her way to the vacant place as she answered. "She's fine. Her nephew is staying with her and I've invited him over for tea."

The family glanced around at one another; it was some time since a lad had come to tea on a Sunday.

Mam answered. "Alice, is that young Tommy? Someone said they had seen him at the corner shop."

Lizzie answered this time, with a sarcastic tone in her voice. "Yes, that's him, Mam. Alice walked home with him after the dance on Saturday."

Mam decided to put Lizzie in her place and said, "That's funny, she walked in with you."

Everyone started laughing and the joke was on her.

Lizzie forked her food around and decided it was best to let the subject drop.

After the meal, Hannah followed Mam into the kitchen. "Mam," she said, "I wanted to have a word with you and Dad when everyone's out."

Mam looked at Hannah. "Something wrong, hen?"

"Oh no, Geordie and me just have something to put to you and me Dad."

Mam looked a bit puzzled as she nodded her head.

Once the house was back in ship shape, the baking started in the kitchen. The smell of the rising bread and baking scones was filling the household. Mam decided she would bake a sly cake and two apple pies, as they were to have company. Mam never found cooking a chore. She had plenty of helpers and all the talking helped the afternoon's work pass very quickly. It wasn't too long before the table began to be filled again with the home baking.

Alice watched the clock all afternoon and finally got up the courage to ask the question, "Mam, can I get out the best china? I want to make our guest welcome."

"I'm sure you do, hen," Mam said with a gentle smile. "Go on."

At half past four, on the dot, Tommy was knocking at the back kitchen door.

Mam shouted with a friendly tone. "Come on in, hinney, it's open."

Tommy very slowly and shyly opened the door. His tall frame made him conscious and he felt himself stooping as he walked into the wonderful smells of Mam's cooking. He wasn't trying to impress her when the words flowed out. "It smells great in here."

Everyone smiled, knowing he'd won Mam over before he set another foot forward. A space was made at the end of the table next to Alice. At first there was a silence, but it was not too long before Tommy was bombarded with questions. It was great to have a visitor from down country and who worked on the farms instead of the mines.

Eventually, Tommy relaxed. He thought to himself, I am home.

As the night wore on and the family began to leave, Mam remembered Hannah wanted to have a word. She was holding back and it appeared that young Dorothy was waiting too.

Mam reached inside her pinny for her cigarettes as she sat next to the fire, opposite Dad. The girls sat on the couch with Geordie in the middle. Hannah was pleased Gracie had decided to take Doreen out for a walk in her pram.

"Well, lasses, what is it?"

Hannah took the initiative to answer. "Well, Mam, we've all been having a talk, I mean me and Dorothy and Geordie."

Dad put his paper down on the floor and turned to listen.

"You know me and Geordie can't have any more children…" Hannah said, "due to me problems having Doreen… and, well, we want to adopt the baby Dorothy has."

•

Chapter 7

Mam and Dad just stared at the three of them.

Hannah continued, "Dorothy could go down to Coventry and stay with our Sadie until the bairn is born and then we can go and collect it. No one would know the truth, they'd just think we'd adopted because we couldn't have any more."

Dorothy kept quiet and continued to watch her mother. Geordie sat swirling his thumbs around each other. He kept looking down at them with the occasional glance at Dad.

Hannah again added, "It'll be for the best, Mam."

At this final remark, Mam sat bolt upright. "So you think it's for the best, do you? The best for who? Who, I ask you?" She paused. "Dorothy? When she sets eye on you with her bairn every Sunday? Geordie?" She paused again, knowing the truth. "Or is it you, me lass?" Mam took a breath. "Now let me tell you, that's Dorothy's bairn and it will know its mother. I know it's shame, but we're a family and families stick together. Now we'll look after her until the bairn's born and then it's up to her. She'll be scrubbing hospital floors the rest of her life to keep it. She's made a bed and by God she'll lie in it." Mam stood up, her piece said, and she walked out into the back yard, slamming the kitchen door behind her.

Dorothy stood. She couldn't hold back the tears and ran upstairs.

Hannah turned her head towards her Dad and said, "I only wanted to help, Dad."

Dad looked at Hannah and Geordie perched on the couch and quietly gave his reply. "You better be satisfied with your lot, lass. Dorothy's going to have enough to think about without shirking her responsibilities. Now you better get your things together. There's dampness in the air for that bairn outside. She needs to be in her own bed."

Geordie got up first. "Come on, pet, we better go," he said, looking down at Hannah. Her head was looking down into her lap, wondering how her good idea had gone so wrong.

All that week, Alice and Lizzie talked over their excitement for the weekend to come. Neither sister really listened to the other. They just wanted to air their thoughts and opinions.

Lizzie confided in Alice, saying, "Billy Jackson's not that bad looking. I mean, he's alright, but well, he's no oil painting, is he?"

Alice's replied, "Yes, he's okay but Tommy is everything I could wish for. I hope we never fall out. Last night I think he wanted to talk about our future together, but his Aunt Bella seemed to be listening and he cut it short."

Lizzie went on, "Billy goes to the wrestling regular with his brother and pals. Last week he said Dave Armstrong is the best wrestler he'd ever seen."

As for the lad at the biscuit factory, Lizzie had all but forgotten him until Friday, payday.

Mrs Butterworth called over to Lizzie again. "Here, you, Lizzie! The post's playing up again. Another letter for the factory, a big one too." She shook her head, looking at the address. "He wants his eyes testing, that postman. I don't know how they keep their jobs. Come on, lass," she said, handing it to Lizzie. "Get ya self over there."

Lizzie took hold of the envelope and made her way out of the shop. Sure enough, that lad was there, checking a delivery from one of the biscuit vans.

"Hello again," he said. "It's Nancy with the laughing face."

Lizzie showed her annoyance as she handed him the letter. "Me name's not Nancy, it's Lizzie."

He beamed. "At last," he said, triumphant, "I know your name. I only said Nancy after the song... you have such a lovely smile."

Lizzie could not hold back her delight. He was very forward but somehow she could not resist his charm.

He gave a slight bow and held out his hand. "I'm Jimmy."

She could hardly breathe as she held out hers to shake his hand. He had a firm grip and she raised her eyes as she gripped back with as much strength.

He grinned. "Are you busy this weekend?"

She replied, "I'm going to the wrestling on Saturday. Have you ever been, Jimmy?"

He was very self-assured and his manner was very bold. It made Lizzie think he was much older than her.

He said, "Of course I've been to the wrestling, it's one of my favourite afternoons."

Lizzie felt she would never get one over him. He's probably been to the Newcastle dance halls as well, she thought to herself. "Well, I'm looking forward to it. I've never been before."

Jimmy's voice was laughing now. "You haven't lived, Lizzie. Let me take you out sometime."

Lizzie took a deep breath. "In your dreams," she said as she turned away to hide her red-faced embarrassment.

Jimmy was not to be deterred, he liked a conquest. He shouted after her, "If you change your mind, you know where I am." He smiled down at his paperwork. He could wait, he thought, especially for one as special as Lizzie.

Lizzie walked briskly back into the shop. She wished he didn't interest her so much. It was far easier being with Billy Jackson and decided to keep her mind on Saturday and going to the wrestling.

Mrs Butterworth had just got one of the girls to lift the butter barrel on the shelf of the counter. "Come on," she shouted over to Lizzie, "you might as well get used to measuring now for when you start serving. I want you to carefully take these rings off the barrels… we keep these for the customers at Christmas. They make garlands out of them for decoration."

Lizzie turned and smiled at Mrs B.

"Now," she said, "we do our measuring on a Monday and Wednesday, after you girls have finished your jobs.

We measure sugar, peas, lentils and yeast. The girls will keep you right on the amounts." She handed Lizzie a square-shaped knife with no sharp corners, and told her to scrape off a four ounces. "Now, Lizzie," she said, "Mrs Millet comes in every Monday at half past three for her butter and today I want you to serve her."

Lizzie stuck the knife into the butter and guessed at what she thought four ounces would look like. Mrs Butterworth smiled. "Yes, that looks about right. Now careful…" She took a breath. "Take it over to the scales and put the quarter ounce weight on."

Lizzie had seen this done hundreds of times whilst shopping with her Mam, but doing it yourself felt really strange. It was not helping the situation having all the girls watching. The only consolation she had was that the shop had no customers in it. Right, she thought to herself, I have to get this right or I'll never get to serve the customers.

She looked carefully now at the scales, taking a small slice of butter off to make the scales balance.

"That's it," said Mrs Butterworth in a booming voice. "That'll do fine. Now take it off and wrap it up carefully in the greaseproof paper. Now then, I'll show you how to fold in the corners, so as no butter is showing. It's the same for everything… no corners showing to stop it seeping out. Tomorrow I'll show you how to fold the sugar packet. Come on, lass, we haven't got all day. Mrs Millet will be here any minute."

The rest of the girls laughed and sniggered, not at

Lizzie, but the fact that they had been through this entire rigmarole when they were learning.

Lizzie and Alice were glad to be walking home that night. Lizzie was pretty quiet. Measuring the butter must have taken it out of her, Alice thought to herself. Although on second thoughts, she thought Mrs Butterworth might have had something to do with it. She could remember when she first started working in the store, everything had to be done so proper. But once you started serving well you wondered what all the fuss had been about.

On reaching the back yard gate, Lizzie asked, "Are you out tonight, Alice?"

"Yes, I'm seeing Tommy. What about you?"

"Oh, I think I'll be having an early night. To tell you the truth, I feel shattered after today."

The girls opened the door to the smell of mince and dumplings.

"Well, have a good night, Alice. I'm straight to bed after me tea."

After dinner, and after the dishes were washed and cleared away, Alice spent a bit of time in the kitchen getting washed and making sure her make-up was perfect. Alice was the first in the house to use Max Factor, pan stick, instead of powder. Her sisters thought it looked a bit orange and you could see what looked like a tidemark. But Alice thought it made her look healthy, just as if she had been in the sunshine all week. She had arranged to meet Tommy at the Golden Lion, and then they were to go on to the Miners' Hall dance.

She sang to herself on the way along the road to the public house. She could see Tommy in the distance, waving and smiling at her. She instinctively waved back and almost felt like running towards him. He made her feel so happy. Tommy kissed her on the lips as soon as they met.

"Where have you been?" he said. "I was getting worried."

Alice turned her head to one side. "Tommy, I'm not late. You must have been early!"

He smiled at her. He got anxious when he thought about her, and he could not help himself. He took hold of her hand and led her into the lounge bar.

"Can we just have one drink here, Alice? There's something I want to ask you, before we get to the dance and all the noise."

"Yes, of course," said Alice, wondering what it could be. She fancied a shandy, but Tommy said to have something special, so she asked for a Martini.

As Tommy returned to their table, he said, "Alice, you always look so beautiful." He sat down and handed her the Martini. "Is that alright for you?"

"Yes, Tommy," she said. "It's fine. What did you want to talk to me about?"

"Well," said Tommy, hoping he would not stutter. "I've been thinking for some time now, and well, I'm hoping you're feeling the same way. You see, Alice..." Tommy looked into his lap, afraid of rejection and what he would do if she said no. "I was hoping we could get together…"

Alice looked at him. "We are together, Tommy, very together I would say."

Tommy felt frustrated. "Alice, I mean really together, like getting married. What about it?"

Alice's jaw dropped. This was really sudden, and this was the last thing she expected. She'd thought he would ask her to seriously 'go courting' and then pop the question after about three years, but not three weeks! What came as more of a surprise to her was her own reply. "Yes, Tommy. If this is your proposal, yes, I accept."

They flung their arms around each other, while the locals watched, smiling and glancing at each other while remembering their own youth. Alice felt in another world as she pulled gently away from Tommy. She looked straight into his eyes and announced, "We'll tell the family next Sunday. I'll tell Mam you're coming for your dinner, and we'll surprise everyone."

Tommy looked directly into Alice's eyes. "Whatever you say, pet," and with that, they stood up and made their way to the dance to celebrate.

Lizzie could not believe how quickly Saturday came around. Everyone in the household felt very excited for her as she was going to Newcastle to see the wrestling. She spent ages raking amongst her sisters' clothes looking for something to wear.

"I've got no idea what folk wear to wrestling matches,"

she said, looking at her sisters from one to another. "What do you all think?"

Various suggestions were made but in the end Lizzie settled for a white shirt waster blouse and a red fully gathered shirt. Mam looked her daughter up and down and nodded in approval. "Shows off that waist of yours, our Lizzie. You look just fine."

Lizzie smiled. "Thanks, Mam." She needed to hear those few kind words.

She walked down towards Boldon Lane to catch the trolley bus into the market. She kept up a brisk walk, until she heard a voice behind her shouting her name. When Lizzie looked around, it was Kitty.

"Hang on a minute, Lizzie," she shouted. "Are you getting the bus into town?"

Lizzie called back to her, "Yes, I'm meeting Billy Jackson for the train to Newcastle, and we're going to the wrestling."

Kitty caught up to Lizzie and said, "I don't believe it, so am I! I'm meeting one of their pals. They must all get the same train up together. I was hoping there would be a girl in the company. I can't believe it's you, that's great."

They both smiled and Kitty linked in with Lizzie's arm. Neither of the girls had been to a wrestling match before and both were really excited.

Very soon they reached the station. Billy was looking at his pocket watch when Lizzie shouted over to him.

He looked up, smiling. "Oh, Lizzie, it's great to see you. I was getting worried you may not come!"

"Wouldn't miss today, Billy," she said.

Billy added, "I've got some good news for Tommy, your Alice's fella. My uncle can give him a start on some building work he has."

Lizzie couldn't stop looking around at all the people waiting for the train. "Thanks, Billy. I'll tell Alice when I get home."

Billy looked deliberately at her. "Well, I was hoping to come back with you, if that's alright?"

"Oh yes," she said, not thinking, "that will be fine."

They all got onto the train. Billy had already purchased a return for Lizzie, which was just as well as she had not given a ticket a thought. They climbed aboard the train and looked along the corridors to find a seat.

When they arrived at Newcastle, Lizzie was taken back with noise and the bustle of the crowds getting to their trains and destinations. It was so exciting Lizzie thought it would take her breath away. She suddenly felt quite small, unable to take in all the beautiful Victorian buildings with the beautiful square-paned windows and huge ornate doors with brass knockers. She was surprised that she had taken notice, she was certainly never aware of buildings in South Shields, other than the Town Hall of course.

Billy was busy taking charge, directing the party in the direction of St James' Hall.

"Dave Armstrong is wrestling Bert Assirati," he shouted as he turned around slightly to check that they were still following him.

The girls glanced at each with a wry smile, not really

knowing what to expect. Soon they arrived and had to join the long queue waiting to have their tickets checked out. Lizzie could feel Billy's excitement as he had unconsciously taken hold of her hand and was squeezing it spasmodically as he moved forward, pulling her gently towards the huge open doors.

Lizzie looked up at the billboards advertising the famous names of the wrestlers. The atmosphere seemed like an anti-climax as they approached the men looking down at tickets to check the date. The event was taking its toll on Lizzie and she felt herself taking in a deep breath wondering what to expect.

"Come on, Lizzie, we're in." Billy pulled on her hand as he guided her to their seats. They were four rows from the front, the noise deafening as people shouted to be heard above the rest. Lizzie could smell the heat of bodies as she meekly sat down along with the crowd that had come with them.

Billy turned to Lizzie with his eyes blazing. "You'll love it when they get started. Oh, look, here he comes..."

The crowds roared and booed at the same time. Lizzie thought her ears would burst. Dave Armstrong strutted his stuff around the four corners of the ring, making gestures at the crowd, which only made them shout louder. Then out came Bert Assirati. The crowd went ballistic when this huge man lifted up the middle rope to the top one and climbed into the ring. Assirati went straight to the middle and with his huge hands resting on his trunks, he glared at Armstrong and shook his head from side to side as if to indicate he had no chance with him today.

The referee took control and told the two men to come into the middle of the floor where he seemed to whisper to each of them some rules they had to abide by. Lizzie laughed to herself at this point as she watched this little skinny man who was dwarfed by the two men he had to control. The referee put his right hand in the air, the two wrestlers turned towards their corners and on reaching them, looked around to see the ref drop his arm as the bell rang loudly. In an instant, the wrestlers lurched forward, raising their arms to lock together to check out each other's strength.

The crowds hurled abuse at them to get on with it. And immediately Armstrong ran for the ropes. He turned, throwing himself into the middle with such force they catapulted him towards Assirati, who was waiting with his expanding stomach laughing as Armstrong bounced off onto the floor. Assirati then dived like a whale on top of him, covering his shoulders. He quickly glanced around for the ref who was now landing on all fours, raising one arm from air to floor counting in a long loud tone, "ONE... TWO... THREE."

Billy jumped to his feet, shouting with the rest of the crowd. As Lizzie stood up, she could see two old biddies in the front row getting to their feet and shaking an umbrella each through the ropes at Assirati. They were shouting abuse that she could not make out due to the noise surrounding her.

The excitement went on and on. Lizzie found it hard to believe how quickly the time passed and soon they were all making their way back towards the train station.

They held hands and Billy kicked a few stones as he walked along with his head down, smiling at the great afternoon they had had together. Lizzie could hardly speak. She thought she had lost her voice when she turned to agree with Billy.

The next few months seemed a whirlwind in the Thompson family. Alice and Tommy were to marry in the registry office in South Shields. He was now settled in the bricklaying job that Billy had arranged for him with his uncle. They would live in Aunt Bella's house. Mam was not too worried about her daughter looking after an elderly relative. Bella did not have long for this world and she was a kindly soul who never hurt a fly. She liked Tommy; he was proving to be a hard-working young man and Mam knew he would make Alice a good husband. He had eyes for no one else but Alice, all around him could see that.

Time was getting near to Dorothy having her baby and Mam watched worriedly as her daughter went out to work every day, never complaining about all the floors and toilets she scrubbed at the hospital. She had to put up with the gossip and Mam sensed the family were becoming outcasts in the community. She never once acknowledged this and if she thought anyone spoke unkindly of her daughter, she promptly put them in their place by tapping their shoulder and saying unashamedly, "That's my daughter you're talking about." They soon turned away and were careful not to speak of young Dorothy when Mam was within earshot.

Dorothy had to leave her hospital job about four weeks before the baby was due. It was becoming obvious to everyone how tired she was, yet she would never fall behind, and worked until her jobs were done. Her boss liked Dorothy. She never spoke ill of anyone and she was very reliable. He thought it was such a shame the father of her baby was not going to marry her. One night he had a quiet word and said, "Dorothy, we can see the work is getting a bit heavy for you now."

Dorothy's big blue eyes widened. "No, I'm fine, Mr Conway."

"Don't worry, Dorothy, your job is here when you're ready to come back. We've never had such a good worker as you. Now you go home and have that baby. When you're up to working, there will always be a place for you."

Dorothy lowered her head and the tears flowed. Mr Conway wanted to cuddle her but he felt it would not be appropriate so uncomfortably he stood up and said, "Now, you take as long as you like to pull yourself together. You call in and see me when you want to take your job up again and we'll make a place for you. Cheerio, Dorothy." He leaned over and patted her gently on one shoulder.

As he shut the door, Dorothy sobbed uncontrollably.

This was the last tear Dorothy was ever to cry again.

The household was buzzing with excitement for her. The girls had been very productive over the last few months. Knitting and sewing had taken up a great deal of their spare time. The only sister who did not knit was Lizzie, however she was very quick to offer to buy a cot for Dorothy. One of the girls at the shop was selling one on behalf of her own sister and Lizzie was the first to snap up the bargain. Eventually the girls in the shop heard about the scandal of Alice and Lizzie's sister. The sombre news came from Mrs Butterworth. She called the girls to attention before the shop opened one morning and made the announcement. She said it was coming from within these four walls first and if anyone had any comments to make, they were to make them now. Otherwise anyone heard making snide remarks after would have her to contend with.

At first Lizzie and Alice were horrified the family secret was brought out in the open like this. But from that moment on, the girls felt free to share their excitement with the others and even Mrs Butterworth said she would be knitting Dorothy a shawl.

"It was said," Alice whispered under her breath to Lizzie on the way home, "that Mrs Butterworth had a love child adopted when she was seventeen years old. It was said she was sent to a convent to have it and the nuns took care of it!"

"No!" said Lizzie. "Who told you that?"

"Oh, it's just talk, but you know there's no smoke without fire. That's why she's probably being so considerate to us!"

"Well, I don't care," said Lizzie, "as long as she's nice."

After that, there was no more gossip.

Dorothy gave birth to a little boy she named Jack... the Thompson family was expanding.

Chapter 8

For the next three years, Lizzie carried on working in Moores Stores. She liked it there. She knew all the customers and their business, and always had a joke with the men folk. She'd come a long way from the young girl she'd been when she'd left school.

On the romantic front though, it was inevitable that she'd get bored with Billy. He was kind and generous, taking her out and always trying to please her, but in the end when he asked her to get engaged he knew that she would refuse. He cried and Lizzie almost changed her mind, but that was not in her nature. She would not back down and she knew Billy was not for her.

Single again, she was enjoying her Friday and Saturday nights in the Mission to Seafarers Hall. She thought this was the best thing her friend Kitty had ever talked her into. They socialised and danced the night away. Lizzie's fun loving, outgoing nature came into its own mixing with men making the most of their time in port. Local lads came along too and on one of these evenings she felt Kitty give her a sharp poke in the ribs.

"Don't look now, kid, Jimmy Smith's just walked in with Robert Walsh, no doubt looking for a good time."

Lizzie felt her heart skip a beat and her throat went dry

as she tried to comment to Kitty. Lizzie and Jimmy had been making snide remarks to each other every time their paths crossed between the shop and the factory.

Jimmy immediately spotted Lizzie. "I know that pretty face," he said, "I'm surprised to see you here." He paused then added, "You don't work here, do you?'

Lizzie took the bait and defended her position, however this time Jimmy stood back and listened. This would be the first time he had her alone on his type of turf, and he decided he would take his chance tonight and see if he could get off with her. He smiled and ordered drinks, and asked her to dance. She agreed.

Most of all, he was polite in his conversation, as he did not wish the evening to end. Finally, he asked her if she would mind if he waited outside to escort her home. Lizzie could not refuse; she had waited three years for this moment. She knew Kitty would be furious. Jimmy had a reputation that went before him.

Kitty squinted her eyes and stared for a moment at her friend. "Makes no difference what I say. You'll do what you want anyway, so I'll see you tomorrow night, kidder. Don't do anything I wouldn't do."

The girls laughed. Lizzie picked her coat from the cloakroom and made her way out to meet Jimmy.

He was leaning up against the wall in the lane when Lizzie came outside. He called her name and as she turned around, she watched him stub out his cigarette on the ground, twisting his shoe on top of it. He walked towards her, smiling, and took hold of her hand. She felt that skip of a heartbeat again and smiled that this moment had finally come.

"I'm parked over here, Lizzie," he stated, pointing down the cobblestoned street.

Lizzie was impressed he had a car, not many lads owned a car in South Shields. But of course she would not acknowledge this and continued walking carefully over the cobbles, trying not to catch the heel of her shoe in the gaps.

"At last I've got you to myself," he said. "You know, I've wanted to ask you for a date for a long time but you're always with a crowd from that shop." He casually opened the car door for her and she climbed inside.

As he walked around the car, she glanced and noticed how clean it was inside. As he got into the driving seat, the words which she had carefully avoided came straight out. "How come you've got a car? Not many lads have a car in Shields."

Jimmy said he wasn't sure about that and told her he'd always owned a car since coming out of the army. Lizzie lifted her head as if to nod and then turned, looking out of the car window deep in her thoughts.

Jimmy headed for Boldon Lane. He knew she lived near the shop as she had said in the past she always walked to work.

Lizzie slowly turned her head and asked him about the army. Jimmy was noncommittal, saying he was a butcher by trade and that he was in London during the blitz, and then quite suddenly, he changed the subject, asking her for directions to her house.

"I live in Gerald Street."

As she said this, he gave a wry smile. "The pit houses! Are you from a pit family?"

Lizzie again went on the defensive. "Yes! So what? What's wrong with the pit and pit families?"

Jimmy laughed. Not again, he thought to himself, and quickly put in that he meant nothing by it although secretly he looked down on pitmen. He hated the thought of the dirt and dust covered bodies he saw at the bus stops waiting for the trolley buses on Westoe Bridges to take them home. He could never imagine getting into a tin tub every night to wash off all that coal dust.

There wasn't much conversation after that and they were both beginning to wonder if they would see each other again. Lizzie spoke first indicating to Jimmy the turning and to stop before they came to her street corner.

"This will be fine here, Jimmy. I don't want to wake anyone with car doors banging."

Jimmy turned to her. "I'd like to take you out, Lizzie. Would you like to go to the flicks tomorrow night? One of my mates said the Humphrey Bogart film is great. How about it? I can come and pick you up if you like."

Lizzie quickly answered, "No! I mean, yes, well, actually yes, I'd like to go but I'll meet you somewhere."

Jimmy told her the picture was at the Palace so they arranged to meet at the corner of Frederick Street the following evening. He sat back in his seat. He was not going to risk trying to kiss her. Lizzie smiled, wishing he had but quickly got out of the car, closing the door gently as she wanted to keep the noise down, avoiding any neighbours looking out of their window. She did not want to be the subject of idle gossip in the corner shop in the morning.

That date was the beginning of a whirlwind romance, which involved dancing and meeting his friends for drinks in pubs around the town. Wrestling matches were a firm favourite on Saturday nights and the pictures were a great place for courting in the back row. Lizzie fell head over heels in love with Jimmy Smith. She did not care that he was ten years older than her or that he had been married, divorced, and was a Catholic.

However, Lizzie's family did not approve. On the first meeting, Lizzie's mother took one look at this handsome young man and took an instant dislike to him. She did not like his sharp suits, highly polished shoes, clean white handkerchief in his top pocket and all his different silk ties. Takes far too much interest in himself to care for her daughter's needs, she thought, and she made no bones about letting that be known. She would not refer to him by name and always called him 'Gentleman Jim'.

In time, Jimmy refused to go into the house and waited in the car, tooting the horn twice until he watched Lizzie skipping happily down the path to meet him.

Lizzie met Jimmy's parents and found them very sombre. His father said hello but made no conversation.

He was totally dominated by his wife, who he always referred to as 'Mother'. She was called Mary and was a different kettle of fish. She watched every move Lizzie made and would hold polite conversation, but Lizzie knew she would never have a friend in this woman.

One night Jimmy held Lizzie in his arms and stated how much he hated living in his parent's house. He told her how happy he was with her and that he wanted them to be together all the time. Lizzie took a deep breath and said she felt the same. Jimmy then asked her marry him. She stared at him as he spilled out his plans and that he knew a flat he could rent in Hartington Terrace. He could get a license and they could be married within three weeks. Lizzie's wide expression and excitement could not be restrained.

"We'll tell me Mam and Dad tonight," she said.

Jimmy pulled away this time. "No, Lizzie, I don't think I'm very popular with your Mam. You better break the ice and let me know when I pick you up tomorrow what they have to say."

Lizzie smiled. She knew no one in the family would be pleased for her, which made her feel sad as she thought they had not even given him a chance.

The following day she told Jimmy she would stay in to wash her hair. This would give her a chance to tell her Mam and Dad the news. When she got in from work, she let it be known she was washing her hair. Mam said it was all right as she would have the kitchen to herself as everyone had plans.

Great, Lizzie thought to herself, that means Dad will have his nap in front of the fire instead of going upstairs to bed for an hour.

By the time the kitchen was cleared of dishes and the family departed, she filled the huge black kettle with water to boil on the stove. She placed a clean towel, soap and shampoo within her reach and went upstairs to change into her dressing gown. Mam and Dad had no idea what she had to tell them. Secretly her Mam had hoped that Jimmy would tire of her young daughter and find someone his own age and religion.

But that was exactly what Jimmy liked about Lizzie. He thought he could make her into what he wanted, which was someone to look after him, keep his home immaculate, cook for him and eventually give him a family. Lizzie came from a big family so he took it for granted she would be able to darn and sew, even make her own clothes. He imagined all her sisters had a rota for cleaning jobs, which they would take a pride in. He presumed she would be a very good cook. On top it all, she was very attractive and very good company with all his friends. Robbie Walsh had told him he had a good catch in Lizzie. What more could he ask for?

When Lizzie finished the final rinse on her hair, she wrapped her head tightly in the towel and continued to wash herself down in the privacy of the kitchen. She began to feel much better and able to face her parents with the news she would be getting married. She made her way into the front room and sat on the little cracket in front of the fire. Dad was leaning back in his rocky chair dozing and Mam continued to read the Gazette for the news in the town.

Lizzie removed the towel from her head and leaned forward to feel the heat of the fire dry her hair.

Eventually after combing it through until she felt it was almost dry, she turned to her mother and said, "Mam, I need to talk to you. It's important."

Mam placed the paper on her lap and, looking at her daughter, she waited for her to speak again.

"Well…" Lizzie paused. "I'm going to get married to Jimmy!"

There was no immediate response to her important statement. Her mother stared with a sadness, looking at her as if watching a lamb to the slaughter. She knew there was no point in arguing with her strong-willed daughter. Apart from the fact she was now over eighteen years old, Lizzie was too much like her and would do as she pleased.

Finally, Mam replied in that familiar low toned disapproving manner. "You'll live to regret that, me lass, but you'll do as you please. You make your bed and you lie in it," and with that final remark she got up, placed the newspaper behind her on the armchair and went in the yard for a breath of fresh air and a smoke to clear her head.

Lizzie turned to her Dad. She knew he had sat up to take notice.

"Nowt to do with me, lass," he said to answer the look on her face. "You're old enough to make your own way.

Can't say as I'm pleased, he's too much of a dark horse. But as I say, nowt to do with me, I just hope you know what you're doing."

Lizzie sat crouched on the cracket. She had a sick feeling in her stomach but thought, what do they know anyway? They had never been long enough in his company. He treated her well and made her very happy. She would marry Jimmy Smith and live in the flat at Hartington Terrace.

The following month Lizzie married Jimmy at South Shields registry office. Neither of their parents attended. Jimmy's mother Mary would not recognise the marriage due to her son being a divorced man. As far as she was concerned Catholics did not divorce and remarry on a whim. His father kept the peace by nodding his agreement as he always did in these situations. Lizzie's mother felt much the same, stating she was not a hypocrite and was too busy that day.

Lizzie was too happy to worry who attended. She had two of her sisters there and lots of Jimmy's friends. Kitty Patterson was her maid of honour and the sun was out. Who could ask for more, she thought to herself. I'd much rather have people around me who wished me well, than family putting the dampers on things.

The happy couple moved into Hartington Terrace. They managed to furnish it from second hand shops, and one of Jimmy's aunts had recently died so her house helped them complete their home. They continued with their jobs and socialised every weekend with friends in the busy bars in the town. Every now and then they would go into Newcastle for a great night watching the wrestling matches, which Lizzie loved.

Her Mam might have been being sceptical in her choice of nickname, but Jimmy really was an absolute gentleman... hardworking, charming, always well turned out, and everything Lizzie needed in a husband. Life was everything she wanted it to be.

But after a couple of years, Lizzie began to get broody. She dropped as many hints as she could to Jimmy who eventually had to give in, even though he had his many doubts... he knew all too well how a child could change your life.

When Lizzie became pregnant, she wanted her mother to be the first in the family to know. Surely this would bring them all together.

"Come on, Jimmy," she said, "come to me Mam's on Sunday. I'm sure they'll all be pleased as punch for us!"

Jimmy looked at her disheartened. "Look, Liz, I know it will make you happy, but they can't stand me. I don't want to go back into that house."

Lizzie's eyes dropped. "It would only be the once and, look, if they don't make you feel welcome, I'll leave the house with you."

Jimmy felt trapped but had to agree. At least this would prove a point once and for all.

It was a beautiful August morning and they decided they would walk to Gerald Street. Jimmy hated walking, he much preferred travelling in his car, but it was a lovely day and it would do Lizzie good in the early stages of her pregnancy to get some exercise.

When they reached the back lane of Gerald Street, Lizzie could hardly retain her excitement and began to quicken her step as they approached the back gate of her parents' house. She reached out for the latch of the gate and stepped into the yard, instinctively looking around for Jimmy and smiling as she did so with apprehension in the meeting of her family that was soon to follow.

She paused for a moment, looking into his eye and said, "Are you ready?"

He smiled, knowing all too well this would not be as pleasant as she imagined. He shrugged his shoulder and followed.

"Mam!" she shouted through the back door as she pulled down on the latch.

Inside, the household came to a silence.

"It's our Lizzie," Gracie squealed, as she hadn't seen her for weeks. She was the first to run into the back kitchen to greet her sister. "Where've you been? We've all been wondering what's happening to you, you haven't been up for ages!"

"Well, I'm here now," said Lizzie in a dismissive tone. She wanted today to go well, not be quizzed about her lack of visiting. She strolled into the front room, looking around at her family as she did so. She felt comfortable as she looked from one to another and wondered why she had stayed away so long. She then remembered Jimmy was with her and turned to pull him by the hand into the family group. "We've got something to tell you!"

All the family stared, waiting in silence for Lizzie to continue. All except Mam. She knew exactly what Lizzie was about to say and she had been dreading this moment coming since her daughter married Jimmy Smith.

"Well…" Lizzie said, dragging out the word. "I'm pregnant." She announced it and jumped into the air with radiant pleasure.

Jimmy looked down at his feet, waiting for some comment to follow and wondering if he had had anything to do with this forthcoming event.

Lizzie turned to him, smiling. "We're so pleased, aren't we, Jimmy?"

He nodded, very aware that her mother's eyes were fixed on him. This made him smile. He knew she was not pleased, which made him all the more determined to pretend he was delighted. The family got up one by one and, with arms outstretched, cuddled Lizzie, expressing their pleasure.

Her mother broke the group by pushing her way into the kitchen and announcing she would prepare some extra vegetables for the dinner table.

Lizzie told Jimmy to sit down next to Hannah and Geordie; she knew they would include him in their conversation. Jimmy sat down and when she was sure he was settled, she followed her mother into the kitchen. "You don't seem happy for me, Mam?"

Mam carried on scraping at the potato in the palm of her hand. "Like I said to you when you married him, hen, you made your bed." Mam kept her gaze on the potato.

Lizzie felt her stomach sink. She wanted her mother to be pleased for her and had been hoping perhaps that a new baby in the family would endear Jimmy to her Mam.

However, the atmosphere was cold and Lizzie knew it was best to leave her mother scraping the potato.

The house was full of chatter. Lizzie hoped that Jimmy would not be aware of the hostility brewing, but he knew all too well.

Lizzie's pregnancy went well. She bloomed all the way through. Even Jimmy began to think his life would not change too much. When Lizzie went into labour, she turned calmly to him, telling him to go to the phone box and ring the midwife.

Jimmy turned, staring, wanting to jump out of his chair but felt frozen. "Are you sure?" he asked, his eyes opening wide.

"Of course I am. My waters have just broken in the lav, so you better get your skates on."

Jimmy had never moved so quickly in his life. Jumping from the chair, he plunged his hand into his pockets, looking for pennies for the phone. He kissed her quickly and said he'd be back in a shifty. With that, he raced down the stairs of their flat, running along the street, forgetting to put his jacket on. By the time he reached the phone box, his teeth were chattering. He fumbled in his trouser pocket for change and as he placed the money in the top of the phone box, he waited for it to answer.

When he heard the midwife's voice, he quickly pressed button 'A' so that he could mumble out the words in a panicking voice.

"Calm down," said the voice from the other end. "Plenty of time, it's her first. I'll be there shortly."

The phone went dead and Jimmy looked at the mouthpiece, knowing he had done his bit now. He slowly came out of the box into the biting cold wind of a February night. He lifted his shoulders and put his hands into his pockets to try and keep warm until he reached his flat. He took a deep breath as he opened the door, closed it slowly behind and as he climbed the stairs, he knew a new chapter in his life was about to begin.

Chapter 9

Lizzie gave birth to a healthy nine and a half pound baby girl.

"We'll call her Molly after me Mam," she beamed from her sweaty face, pulling herself up to take the baby girl into her arms.

"Have you discussed that with your husband?" said the midwife, smiling as she finally wrapped her newly cleaned little parcel in a white sheet to hand to the new mother.

"Well, not exactly. We thought we would have a boy, but I'm sure Jimmy won't mind. He's never mentioned a girl's name so I suppose I can have my own way."

The midwife looked at Lizzie now in her bedraggled state and announced, "Come on, lass, let me give your face a wipe with the flannel and run the comb through your hair. You want to look your best for your man when you show him that beauty you've got there."

Lizzie looked down at little Molly and smiled, thinking she was quite right. She may have a baby but she did not want to let herself go.

Jimmy came slowly into the bedroom. He looked sheepishly at his wife and asked how she was.

Lizzie beamed. "Piece of cake," she joked. "Would you like to hold your daughter?"

Jimmy approached the bed, not quite sure about all this responsibility which was now being placed upon him. The midwife took charge and took the baby from Lizzie. She told Jimmy to sit down in the chair next to the bed and as he did so, she placed the little girl in his arms.

"Better get used to Molly straight away," the midwife announced. "Your help will be needed for the next two weeks while Lizzie builds her strength up."

Jimmy did not say a word, but 'Molly', he thought to himself, is not going to be her name. I'm calling her Mary after my mother.

When eventually the midwife said it was time for her to leave, Jimmy got up, giving the baby to Lizzie and saying he would see her out. As they reached the landing, Jimmy pulled from his pocket two packets of cigarettes.

"Here," he said. "You've done a good job," and as he handed her the packets she smiled, "Thanks. Just what I need. I'll enjoy a couple to night with my cocoa before I go to bed." And with that, she left.

Jimmy locked the door behind him and went upstairs to be with Lizzie and the new baby.

As he entered the bedroom, Lizzie was looking tired. Giving birth was now taking its toll. Jimmy took the baby from her and just as if he had done this before, he placed the baby into her cot next to Lizzie. As he straightened his back and without looking at Lizzie, he said, "We're calling her Mary after me mother."

Lizzie was too tired to argue and it really did not matter

to her what her daughter was called. She was a beautiful healthy baby. That's all that mattered.

The year that followed was a turning point in Jimmy and Lizzie's married life. No longer could they go out together as and when they pleased, his dinner was never ready on time and Lizzie began to look drab in Jimmy's eyes. Her hair began to look lank and she was never quite clean enough for him due to the baby being sick, or could it be that Lizzie had stopped looking at herself as a woman, now she was a mother.

Jimmy hated this trapped feeling and he could feel himself wanting to get out more and more. He began by telling small white lies... a friend needed to talk about a job, he needed to speak to a friend about their family problems, until eventually he just told her he was going out. He picked up where he had left off his friendship with Robbie Walsh. Although Robert was now married himself, he was always glad to get out of the house. He was married to a very caring woman, but she was too homely for Robert and quite content to spend a night at her mother's house if Robert wanted to have a drink.

"Get yourself away," she would say. "I'll just pop around to me Mam's."

This was a life many Geordie women lived and no one thought ill of it. Men liked a drink after a hard day's work and they were entitled to it, or so the women were led to believe.

Jimmy and Robert always attracted the women, Jimmy

with his handsome dark looks and slicked back hair and Robert with his charming Irish accent, large pale blue eyes which smiled at you with all the attention he could muster. Yes, they had it made where woman were concerned in South Shields. It was not too long before the pair began to have the odd fling on the way home, nothing too serious, just a bit of fun to kill the boredom of married life.

When Mary was eighteen months old, Lizzie announced with glee she was pregnant again. Jimmy was devastated. Although he had begun to love and adore his daughter, he had not wanted another child to care for so soon. He smiled and did his best to say all the right words, but the irritation was beginning to dwell on him. He decided he would have to get away from this domesticity. The only way he could think of was to change his job and become a long distance lorry driver. He made enquiries, got the job and came home one night telling Lizzie he would have to earn more for a new mouth to feed and told Lizzie his change of jobs. Lizzie thought Jimmy was wonderful to care so much about their family and kissed him tenderly.

"Jimmy, I'm so glad I've got you to care for me so much that you would actually take a job working away during the week," she said. "I really love you. We're so lucky and now we're having another baby to make our marriage complete."

Jimmy felt quite smug, getting out of that so well. Now

he could have some freedom during the week and a home life at weekends. It could not have worked out better.

When the new baby was born, Jimmy was in Birmingham with a long distance delivery. He had made himself known in various boarding houses up and down the country. The life suited him well and even when Lizzie said she thought the baby may arrive that week, Jimmy said, "No, you're not due for another week. I'll go to work as normal. If you need anything, your sisters will help and I'll be back on Friday."

Lizzie gave a half smile. She knew she couldn't insist, so she nodded and turned her cheek away from him as she hid the tears coming down her face. She got up and went into the kitchen to put up some bait for her man to take away with him in the early morning. She would still have to get up with him to make his flask, but this little preparation would give her a bit more time in bed before Mary woke for her early morning feed.

The following day, Lizzie knew the baby was coming. She could feel the familiar ache in her bottom back of her back and she was unable to sit with any comfort. She quietly packed a few things for herself and Mary then decided to make her way up to her Mam's. When she arrived, her Mam took one look at her and said, "Well, lass, you're not due for another week but from the look on your face I'd say it's on its way."

Lizzie plonked herself down on the couch, her legs open with her belly resting between her thighs. "Mam,

I'm shattered," she said. "Can I have the baby here? Jimmy went away yesterday and I've no one to look after Mary."

Mam smiled at her daughter, at the same time checking that Mary was still asleep in her pushchair. She was all too pleased to be needed again. No lass should be on her own when she was about to give birth. She told Lizzie she'd make a cuppa and then get the bed ready, and would also pop across to Alice's and get Tommy to phone for the midwife.

"Don't worry, hen, you're home now and I'll take care of you and the bairn."

The rest of the day passed peacefully, but soon the bustle of Dorothy's little 'un young Jack coming in from school got Mary excited. Children recognise children, Mam thought as she watched Mary tug at Jack's shirt tail, which was hanging out of his trousers. Jack was a pleasant child and was happy to sit down on the floor and play with a box that she was investigating. Lizzie was settled upstairs in young Jack's bedroom. He would have to sleep in his mother's room for a few days. This of course was a special treat for him. He was told by his nana he would be the first to see the new baby.

By the time the midwife arrived, Lizzie was well into her labour. She was having a difficult time and was getting very tired. Her red, mottled and blotched face showed her distress. The midwife looked concerned as she struggled to turn the baby's head.

"We may need the doctor," she announced. "But we'll see how you get on."

This remark gave new strength to Lizzie as she took a deep breath to start her work all over again.

"That's it, lass. Keep pushing… keep pushing… now wait, wait…"

Lizzie panted even though she was desperate to push.

"Good lass, the head's out."

Lizzie lay back, taking a breather.

"Now come on, lass, one more push should get this baby out," and with that, Lizzie gave her all with the final effort that her body could muster.

"It's a boy," announced the midwife. "A bit skinny, mind you, not like your first, but a healthy lad."

Lizzie shed a tear as she felt alone in the house that was full of people. She could hear her sisters downstairs, waiting for news as they chatted over cups of tea, but all she could wonder now as she cradled her son was what Jimmy was doing.

Jimmy settled into life on the road like a duck to water. Each of his landladies had something to offer. Betty in Blackpool cooked just like his mother. Ellen from Chester would listen to him for hours into the night, making him feel the most important man in the world, while she thought he wanted her company and secretly hoped one day he would make a pass at her. However, Jimmy saved that side of his needs for a Wednesday night in Birmingham with Rosie. Her bright lipstick, fiery red hair draping over her clinging tops revealing ample breasts encouraged his eye down the pencil skirt, which edged into her nylons and high-heeled shoes. Jimmy loved it when she turned and leaned over to pour out drinks at the start of their evening when he could admire her shapely legs, divided only by the seam in her black stockings. Jimmy was smug in the double life he had managed to get away with so well.

When the weekend came, Jimmy was feeling tired driving home. It had been a long week and the deliveries had been heavy to drops he had not been to previously. He approached Scotch Corner and knew he would be home soon and hoped that a hot dinner would be waiting for him. He dropped off the lorry and got into his Zephyr car, comforted by the familiar surroundings and local Geordie accents, nodding their heads with the occasional, "All right there, mate."

It was just a short journey home from the depot. He got out of the car and slowly walked to the boot to pull out the holdall containing his week's washing. He suddenly felt exhausted as he pushed the key into the door lock.

The house smelled cold; there was no familiar cooking smell, which made him wonder if Lizzie had gone into labour. He quickly went up the stairs of the flat and found the note which she had left for him… 'Gone to Mam's, think I've started, if I'm not here when you get back you will know where I am.'

It was irritating. Jimmy could feel a rage inside of him that he had not experienced before. He never did want children and he was taking second place! He was hungry and as he opened every cupboard door, there was not a bit of food in the house. He leaned over the kitchen bench and as he did was brought straight back up again by his fists banging down from where they had just rested.

"Bloody woman," he shouted. "Not a thought for me out at work all week." He turned and stormed into the bedroom, not knowing what he was looking for. As he slowly came back into the living room, he picked up his coat and decided to go to the fish and chip shop on the corner.

The queue was long, stretching out of the door and making its way across the glass-fronted window. The pubs must be coming out, he thought to himself as his eyes skirted around the line forming through the shop. As he did so, he recognised one face and wondered where he knew her from. She caught him looking and gave a knowing nod. He smiled, trying desperately to work out where he knew her from. He did not have to wait too long. When she'd been served, she stopped and asked how him and Robbie were and said that he hadn't been in the Britannia for a while.

"What ya doing now, Jimmy?" she said.

Jimmy leaned back against the wall of the shop. He raised his knee and placed the back of his foot against the wall. The tiredness had suddenly left him. "Well, I'm working away, but if I'd known you still went down there I would have made more of an effort to get there when I was home."

The girl smiled, wanting the conversation to carry on. "I'll wait for you outside, Jimmy, and you can tell me what you've been up to."

Jimmy nodded to the girl, wondering what her name was and trying to remember the last time he was in the Britannia. When he was served, he picked up his fish and chips and the penny from the counter. He turned, looking outside for the girl who had spoken to him. She had already started eating her chips, hands getting warm from the packet.

Jimmy approached her, hoping he would not have to use her name, when she said, "You don't remember me, do you, Jimmy?"

He quickly put in, "Yes I do, I remember your pretty face, but I'm no good with names." He smiled as he said this, hoping she would help him out. She did and said she was called Lily. She was a chatty girl, a bit dim, he thought, but probably good for a one-night stand.

Jimmy took her back to the flat. He said his wife had left him for another man and that he was devastated. Lily's heart softened. She dropped her empty paper bag of chips in the street outside his front door and reached up to kiss him.

"Don't worry," she said. "I'll help you forget."

Jimmy smiled again. It was so easy for him to pick up girls, but he would have to be careful... this was getting too close to home.

The next morning he got up early and told Lily he had an early shift for the weekend.

"I'm doing overtime," he said, "so you'll have to get yourself away."

The girl stirred slowly from the bed, leaning up and resting on her elbows. She nodded, trying to get herself pulled together from the deep sleep she had been in. As she stretched her knees up and put her feet onto the floor, she muttered, "When will I see you again?"

Jimmy did not answer at first, pretending to get his clothes together. "Oh, I'm not sure. I'm doing a lot of overtime," he said but he then gathered his thoughts and added, "Probably see you next time I'm in the Britannia."

Lily had heard this all before and knew it was over before it began. "Yes, alright, Jimmy, see you around then." She put on her clothes, picked up her handbag where she dropped it on the way up the stairs and left.

Jimmy looked around the bombsite and made an effort to get rid of the evidence. He quickly opened all the windows to get rid of any tell-tale smells. He knew he had no time to wash the sheets so he hoped a good airing would do the trick. He got out the carpet sweeper and glided over the carpet pieces that were placed around the rooms. The polish tin still had a scraping around the edges so he got out what he could to make the room smell clean.

As he did so, he began to notice how shabby the furniture was looking. He found tea stains on the table that he had not noticed before and as he pushed the sweeper around the corners of the room, he could see the collected dust and fluff that must have been there for some time. Lizzie was not the woman he thought he had married. He'd thought that coming from a big family she would be nipping clean, but as he looked around his flat he became disappointed with his lot. He felt trapped again. He could not dwell on these thoughts much longer as he knew he would have to get to Lizzie's mother's to see if she had had the baby.

He left the flat at nine o'clock. It seemed like a good time to get to his mother-in-law's to make him look concerned just enough after having worked all week. When he arrived, he looked up and down the street he hated. Full of pitman's families covered in grime, he thought. He got out of his car, looking flash and smug in the fact he had pulled yet another girl.

He knocked on the door, not normal in families in the pit community – but he wasn't a pitman. Mam rushed to the door, thinking the debt collector must have got the wrong address. As she poked her nose through the gap, she suddenly pulled back in surprise.

"Oh, it's you, Gentleman Jim," she said, voice bitter with scorn. "Come in. Our Lizzie has had the bairn. I don't suppose you know." She looked at Jimmy, waiting for a response while at the same time her eyes looked him up and down with contempt. She wouldn't trust this man if he was the last man on earth. How could a man be working most of the night, be worried his wife wasn't in her bed, nine months pregnant, his daughter missing and look as smart and cool as a cucumber as he did.

Jimmy answered, "Well, I've just not long been back. I had a wash and came straight up."

Mam was glaring at him and said, "Well, lad, she's upstairs. You've got a son. She'll be wanting to show you."

Jimmy walked past Lizzie's mother as if she was part of the furniture. He nodded to his father-in-law as he passed him. Lizzie's Dad nodded back and carried on reading, head buried into his newspaper. Jimmy made his way up the stairs to the back bedroom where he popped his head around the door to find his daughter Mary playing happily on the floor.

He stood for a moment, watching Lizzie feeding her new baby son.

"Jimmy," she screamed with delight, "look, we've got a boy. What'd you want to call him?"

Jimmy looked down at the scene, feeling slightly guilty. "Well, pet, it's up to you. I called the last one."

Lizzie smiled, feeling content. "I like the name Daniel. No one in the family is called that and I think it's a nice name!"

Jimmy answered, "Well, Daniel it is, pet, you have your wish."

Jimmy let the next half hour pass, listening to Lizzie explain the birth and then he said, "When do you think you'll be home? You know I miss you not being there when I get in."

Lizzie smiled as she reached out for his hand. "Jimmy, I've just had the bairn. You can stay here if you like. Me Mam won't mind."

Jimmy pulled away gently from her grip. "No, I don't want to put anyone to any trouble. You just stay as long as it takes and I'll come and get you when you're ready."

Lizzie felt hurt. She'd been hoping her husband would stay, but she knew in her heart that this would not work with her family.

Jimmy stood up, feeling uncomfortable in the knowledge that no one had came upstairs to offer him a cup of tea. He decided to make excuses that he had been driving late into the night due to a road accident holding up the traffic on one of the narrow roads. He assured Lizzie he would be fine and would be back to work on Monday, and told her she was in the best place.

By the time he was home again next weekend, they would both be back in their bed together and would have their children home with them.

Lizzie smiled, contented.

But life would never be the same again. Jimmy knew this as he travelled on the road again with his load.

Chapter 10

Lizzie returned home with the help of her sister Gracie. She was eager to get back to the normal routine of married life. She tried her best to be organised as she knew Jimmy liked this, but in the end she just had to give in, she was unable to cope with the rounds of housework, washing and ironing.

It was more important to her to keep her babies happy, take them out for walks in the pram when they cried and visit her friends to drink tea and talk about the mundane chores of married life, which she enjoyed. Lizzie became very good friends with Robert Walsh's wife, Joyce, and found that she had a lot in common with this gentle woman with two daughters of a similar age to her own children. Once Lizzie began to talk, she realised that Joyce was living the same life as her. She discovered that they were telling very similar stories when their husbands returned home after the boys' nights out they had had together, and began to wonder if all these stories were true, even going so far as to ask if Joyce was feeling the same.

Joyce was a simple woman. She had never thought to question anything in her life and certainly never anything her husband Robbie told her. He was her husband and she had no reason to question him, or was it perhaps she was afraid to.

Lizzie was a different kettle of fish. She was starting to have doubts ever since she returned home and found a lump of discarded hair in her rubbish when she was about to empty it into her bin. She stopped and stared and then slowly picked out this thin piece of blonde hair, which she thought had been removed from a brush. Lizzie had black hair, as did all of her sisters, so she knew it did not belong to any of her own family. She also knew that none of Jimmy's family had blonde hair, so for the first time in her marriage Lizzie felt a sick tingling feeling in the pit of her stomach that she could not explain. She felt insecure. She felt her grip on Jimmy slipping away. No longer did she look forward to him coming home at weekends only to be told by him that he needed time on his own to unwind and would she mind if he popped into the town for a pint with Robbie. Lizzie began to realise it was pointless making a fuss; he would get his own way in the end. However, she was fast becoming angry. She had a fiery temper and was easily roused. She and Jimmy had their fights like everyone, but now the verbal abuse had progressed to a few slaps across the face. She'd been pushed out of his way as he left their flat to meet his mates but now she was aware that his fists were clenched when she challenged him and when finally he lost control, he grabbed her by the throat, pushing her backwards against the wall so that the back of her head took the full force of his weight.

When he let go, her head slumped forward and she could see stars as she regained her balance, watching him slam the front door behind him. She slipped down slowly to her knees, holding her face in her cupped palms. Tears welled in her eyes until she finally picked up the end of her cotton skirt to wipe her face clean. She got up, feeling more angry than ever. She would get to the bottom of all this if it killed her. She was no fool, she told herself as she put some water in the kettle to make some tea. She would have to get someone to watch her children one night so that she could follow him. She slowly poured the water over the tea leaves in her teapot, her mind wondering as she picked up the half full bottle of puro milk which she gently poured into her cup. Her children were asleep in bed and had not been woken by the noise raised by the scene that was still so clear in her mind. What happened to our happy marriage, she thought as she settled into the worn armchair next to the radio. She was so unhappy with her life and could see no way out.

That night when Jimmy returned, she heard the front door slam behind him and listened as he staggered up the stairs. This was not the right time to make a scene, she decided. She would wait until morning. She turned over quietly, facing the bedroom wall to pretend to be asleep. Jimmy crawled into bed and soon she could hear his snoring. It was safe to close her eyes.

In the morning, Jimmy was woken by his children's voices as they played around the flat. He recalled the previous evening's conversation with Robbie Walsh and Jimmy's plans to change his job. His mistresses were getting too demanding on his time. Each of them thought they were the only one and wanted Jimmy to move into their homes and settle with them. Robbie had laughed at his friend's complicated lifestyle and replied, "Jimmy, come and work on the trip buses! You'll be away from home most days and not tied down to a set routine. You'll meet different people and we'll have plenty of time to arrange our nights out together. You know, there's so many women, just waiting out there for us. We can't fail!"

Jimmy remembered how he had leaned back in his chair, taking a drag on his cigarette while his other hand was waiting at the ready with a glass of whisky. Jimmy smiled as he pulled on his trousers and covered his bare chest with his string vest. Yes, he thought to himself, I'll tell Lizzie I want more time at home with me bairns. She'll believe that.

He pulled on the same socks he had taken off the night before and made his way to the kitchen where Lizzie had started to cook his breakfast as she had heard him getting up.

She was still seething from the previous evening. Jimmy could sense the atmosphere and decided to get in first with the news he was going to change his job.

"Morning, pet," he smiled as he leaned towards her to offer a peck on the side of her head.

Lizzie did not respond at first, pretending to be too involved in frying eggs. She ignored him, flipped the egg over and began to dish out the food onto his plate.

"We've already eaten," she remarked as she placed the plate on the table, "and I've got to wash the bairn to go to me Mam's."

Neither of them looked at each as Jimmy sat down. Lizzie picked up her daughter and sat her on the kitchen bench, pulling off the nightdress the child was wearing. She had a dish of water ready and dipped in the flannel to wash her child's face. She couldn't wait any longer and in the comfort of washing the child, she began asking awkward questions that Jimmy did not want to answer.

"Where'd you go last night? You were really late back."

Jimmy opened up his newspaper and balanced the broad sheets between his cup and a bottle of sauce.

Lizzie carried on, "How come you spend so much time with Robbie?" But before she could continue, Jimmy grunted that he never said he was with Robbie.

She glared at him. "Who were you with then? Joyce said Robbie was meeting you!"

Jimmy's irritation was beginning to show but Lizzie had only just started. She went into full throttle and bombarded Jimmy with questions and statements, whilst pointing out the many lies he had told her. She was getting so wound up in the bottled up information, which she had been storing in her head, she did not notice him rise from the chair. Jimmy wanted to lash out at Lizzie but was restricted by his daughter's presence now in her mother's arms. He turned half circle, picked up his breakfast plate and lashed the plate up against the kitchen wall.

Lizzie froze as she looked at the dripping food sliding down the wall. Jimmy took the side of his arm to knock her out of his way and as he did so, Mary screamed in terror as her mother clung to her. This time Lizzie had had enough. She put her child to the floor and went after him to the bedroom, still shouting about the lies and then she finally plucked up the courage to accuse him of having affairs.

Jimmy turned, raising his fist, and with one swing he punched her to the floor.

Lizzie got up straight away and with adrenaline rising she took one full swing back at him. They both grabbed onto each, pulling hair, kicking and screaming. Both children were now at the bedroom door, watching their parents rolling on the floor. The children's screams could be heard outside in the street, though no one dared knock at the door. Lizzie was the first to realise their distress and screamed at Jimmy to stop and look at the bairns.

When he did, the guilt overwhelmed him and he rushed forward to throw his arms around them. "It's alright," he said. "Just having a little fight. Look, we're both alright."

The children calmed down and their sobs gave way to gentle tears. Lizzie slowly rose from the floor, hardly able to lift her limbs from the battering they had taken.

Jimmy turned and snarled at her, "Look what you've done! And here's me trying to get a job that doesn't keep me away from home as much. I must be mad. Look at you, you're a fat slob. I don't know why I stay!"

"Get yourself away," she retorted. "I'll survive. Plenty women do. I don't need you. Go on, get out and see if I care."

Jimmy stood looking at her square on now. If he'd had a knife, he would have killed her. "You don't get me out that easy, Lizzie. This is my house so you bugger off. You're not a woman, look at you!" and with that final remark he spat on the floor.

They stood staring at each other. The children by now had gone into the kitchen to play as if knowing the fight was over.

Jimmy put on a clean shirt from the wardrobe. "Look," he said, "I'm going to have a wash and go down to Robbie's coach depot. They need drivers and I'm going to see if I can get a start."

Lizzie could quite easily have continued to row about the whole business but she was sore and tired and still had to go to her Mam's. She nodded her head in agreement and got ready to walk to her mother's house.

She was aching in every part of her body as she pushed Daniel's pushchair slowly along the road to keep pace with Mary's little legs. The pace suited Lizzie who was finding each step harder to take as she put her muscles through agony walking the two miles to reach her mother's house.

As she reached the back gate, she struggled to keep it open and asked Mary if she could help. Her Mam was watching from the kitchen window and came outside to ask what was wrong. Lizzie looked up to her mother whose face said it all.

"Been bashing you again, has he?"

Lizzie realised the bruising must be coming out now as she tried to avoid Mam's gaze by picking Daniel from his pushchair.

"I'm alright, Mam, don't fuss."

Mam followed her daughter into the house. "You should leave that bastard before he kills you."

Lizzie turned to her Mam and asked, "Would you take me in?"

Mam gazed at her daughter, knowing she was serious. "Well, you know, pet, I could take you in but I've no room for the bairns."

Lizzie dropped her head and looked away as she answered. "Well, don't make comments like that when there's nothing I can do about it. I've got no money, no job and nowhere to go with me bairns." Her voice was firm now. "So, Mam, keep your comments to yourself."

Mam overlooked her daughter's harsh words. She knew the lass was suffering and there was nothing she could do about it. "Come on," she said, "we'll have a cup of tea. You look like you could do with one."

Lizzie felt safe there and enjoyed the chatter of her sisters again as they all met on the same day each week at their Mam's house to catch up on the gossip. Her sisters overlooked her bruised face and cheered her up by enjoying the children happily playing together.

When Lizzie returned home, Jimmy was in good

spirits. He announced he had the job at the bus depot. "I've invited Robbie and Joyce around for tea," he said.

Lizzie looked at his handsome face smiling at her, but before she could answer he added, "I've bought some baker's bread and boiled ham and some cakes for the bairns."

She smiled, knowing some company would ease the air tonight.

And it did. Robbie and Joyce made good company, the children played well together and Jimmy did his best to help in the kitchen and play the perfect husband. Even Lizzie's bruises were explained away, stating she had tripped over some toys in the yard while hanging out some washing.

"She will have to be more careful," joked Jimmy. "Carrying too much washing in the basket, unable to see what's under her feet!" he continued loudly to Robbie so that Joyce could hear.

Joyce took no notice. She would not have made a comment anyway, Lizzie thought to herself as she passed around the sandwich plate.

Jimmy turned away thoughtful as he made this comment. He would have to make sure he kept his fists away from her face. She looked terrible, he thought, much too hard to explain away as an accident if it happened again.

Over the next few weeks, things improved in the household. Jimmy settled into the new routine and was relieved to be finally rid of his mistresses around the country.

News finally came from the council that a three-bedroomed house with a garden was available in Brockley Whins. Lizzie could not hold back her excitement at the thought of the move. They did not have a lot of furniture, but she was used to making do and mending.

When the day finally came to move, there was great excitement. No one in the family had their own garden, she thought as she looked out of her new kitchen at her garden of clay. She walked slowly into the long sitting room, carrying Daniel on her hip. She turned her head from side to side, looking at the windows at both ends of the room. She smiled happily, noticing that they would let the sun shine through no matter what time of day it was. She had two good-sized bedrooms and a small box room for Daniel who would soon need a bed of his own. The main attraction of the mid terrace was a separate bathroom and toilet, which was inside the house. Lizzie looked into the bathroom and toilet every time she went upstairs. No more going outside in the winter or using pots in the night, which had to be emptied in the morning. She smiled a lot in this new house.

Jimmy wasted no time getting to know the neighbours, hoping to come across some nice female face to steal away for some moments together. However, none caught his eye and it was not long again before Jimmy and Robbie sought some excitement in the town once again.

The Friday night out with Robbie soon turned into a

routine, which the two men enjoyed together. Even Lizzie began to get used to a night she could take the children around to spend alternative evenings with Joyce.

It was not long before Jimmy and Robbie's presence was noticed by a couple of local lasses at the Britannia pub. The girls were both married, looking for a bit of fun, but this time it was getting too close to home. Their weekly meetings were noticed around the town and it was not long before the foursome were spotted in the back row of the pictures by an old school chum of Lizzie's who had also moved onto Brockley Whins Estate.

She wasted no time in seeking Lizzie out at the local shop.

"Lizzie," she called out, "I seen your Jimmy the other night in the pictures. I'm sure he and Robbie were with a couple of lasses! Of course could be wrong!" she gloated.

Lizzie turned and gave this gossip a steely look, noticing the curl in the side of her mouth as she completed the sentence. She would not give the woman the satisfaction of the devastation she felt as she realised Jimmy was up to his old tricks again.

She quickly retorted, "Oh, that was my sister and her mate, up from Coventry. We were all supposed to be out together but I couldn't get a babysitter." Lizzie had become an accomplished liar when covering up her husband's indiscretions.

Her old chum made no effort to continue this conversation and simply nodded, disappointed she had to continue with her boring day and look for something to cook for her man's tea when he came in from work.

Lizzie returned home with her children in tow. She felt sadness and anger as she wondered how she could prove Jimmy was playing away. She decided she must have some proof. She knew her suspicions were not enough and needed some evidence.

Chapter 11

Lizzie had become good friends with her new next-door-neighbour, Rosemary. She was a kindly woman who kept her own counsel and never once made remarks about other people on the council estate. Lizzie wanted to take her into her confidence but knew if she did, Rosemary would not assist her in the plan to follow Jimmy. Lizzie would have to lie to gain her assistance in the plan.

She left her children playing in the sitting room, while she popped her head around the neighbour's back kitchen door to ask if she wanted to pop in for a cuppa. Rosemary smiled as she thanked her and slipped her bare feet into the slippers waiting at the back door. They both passed between the openings in the fence joining their houses together. Lizzie went straight to the cooker to turn the gas on and boil up the kettle of water. Rosemary settled down into the kitchen chair and glanced around at the untidy kitchen, so unlike her own. The children came scattering into the kitchen on hearing a different voice. Lizzie turned quickly and told Mary to take Daniel out to play. Mary was a good-natured child and took her brother's hand to lead him out into the front street. There were always children to play with as other like-minded mothers needed to get their brood from under their feet to get on with their chores.

Lizzie opened a packet of custard creams but did not bother with a plate to put them on. She filled the brown teapot with water and placed it next to the biscuits. She turned casually, going to the sink to rinse out a couple of cups.

Rosemary breathed a disapproving sigh and hoped Lizzie had not noticed.

"Well," said Lizzie as she settled opposite her neighbour, wondering how she would approach the favour she needed. "What have you been up to? It seems ages since we've had a cuppa together."

"Nothing much," replied Rosemary as she tried to recall anything interesting. "Well actually, yes, we've been doing a bit of decorating in the little back bedroom. To tell you the truth, it was getting to be a bit of a dumping ground with it being empty. I hate mess so I got Jackie to give me hand and do a bit of painting."

"Oh, that's great. I wish I could get Jimmy to do a bit of painting. We haven't done anything since we moved in!"

Rosemary nodded, knowing that they were unlikely to do so for some time.

Lizzie added that Jimmy was so busy working every hour God sent and she never had a minute spare for decorating. Then she seized the moment. "I wanted to ask you a big favour?"

Rosemary's eyes now peeped over the top of the cup of tea she was drinking, wondering what she needed.

"Well, me Mam's not too good at the moment and me sisters are taking it in turns to go up on a night and get her ready for bed. Me Dad's not been himself lately and me Mam's a bit heavy for him to manage." Lizzie looked directly into Rosemary's eye and said, "Well, you know how independent old women are and me Dad's worried case she takes a fall."

Rosemary smiled at her, feeling she should help out her neighbour in a time of need. Rosemary went to church every week and could not live with herself if she did not practice the preachings of the church. "Yes," she stated, smiling that she could carry out a good deed. "I'd be happy to help you out. Jackie is working nights this week so it will be a bit of company for me, looking after the bairns."

Lizzie relaxed her shoulders back as she leaned into the kitchen chair, content her plan was starting to come together. She wasted no time and asked Rosemary if Friday would be alright. She continued that all her sisters were busy on Friday and it would be a good night for her to take her turn.

"It will only be the once," she said. "I'm sure me Mam will get her strength back. She's a fighter you know. Just the one night, Rosemary, I won't put on you again."

The two neighbours smiled at each other as they finished their cuppa.

"I'll give you a knock on Friday night when I get the bairns settled," said Lizzie. She picked up the teapot and filled their cups again to carry on gossiping about their new houses and the plans they had for them.

Friday came too quickly for Lizzie. She felt edgy as she thought about following Jimmy. She knew his route so well now as Jimmy had often gone through this when he returned home after having one too many. Although, she thought to herself, he never let his indiscretions slip. She would have to find this out for herself.

Jimmy came in from work to his dinner waiting on the table. Lizzie knew his whistle was always loud and clear on a Friday night. She made sure his suit was hanging from the wardrobe door, and had taken great care pressing his shirt, carefully hanging it in front of the suit. She left Jimmy to pick his own tie from his expanding collection draped across the cord that stretched along the inside of the wardrobe door.

Jimmy suspected nothing as he ate his usual Friday night sausage and mash. The only comment he made to Lizzie over the top of his newspaper was to ask if his white shirt was ironed.

Lizzie turned from the kitchen sink. "Yes, pet, and I got your suit out for you."

Jimmy made no comment and carried on reading his newspaper.

She felt sick as she thought about catching the bus into town after him. She turned from her washing up and carefully leaned over him to remove the empty dinner plate.

Jimmy grunted as he moved out of her way. "Can't you wait until I've finished me paper?" He carried on reading not expecting an answer.

Right on cue with the six o'clock radio news, Jimmy got up to leave the table. He ignored Lizzie and the children as he went upstairs for a bath. Lizzie had kept the fire on all day to heat the water up. She wanted to keep everything right and not give him anything to argue over.

Jimmy turned on the bathwater and began to bring out of the bathroom cabinet his shaving brush, soap and razor. He quickly lathered up the soap with the brush and began circular movements around his face until the foam covered the growth of stubble. He carefully took his razor and began to peel away the foam leaving a soft layer of skin beneath it. He quickly shook the razor in the sink, ready for the next action across his face. He was relaxing now as he thought about the night ahead. Robbie had made the arrangements with the girls and every thing was set for them to meet at the Britannia as usual. He bathed, stretching out so that the water could ripple over his chest as he smoothed soap over his hairy body.

He forgot all his responsibilities and he never gave a thought to the needs of his wife and children. Jimmy's only thought was his own needs and pleasure and tonight was his night.

By the time he came downstairs to tell Lizzie he was leaving, she was working herself up to the night ahead. She tried desperately not to let her anxiety show as she sat reading the Gazette, pretending she was in the middle of a paragraph she could not look up from. He popped his head around the door in the sitting room, stating he was off to meet Robbie. Lizzie nodded from the paper, unable to meet his gaze.

As Jimmy closed the front door, she got up to watch him get into his car. He looked immaculate in his Jackson the Tailor's suit, his tie in a tight Windsor knot, pulling together his crisp, clean, white shirt. He looked the perfect gentleman... Gentleman Jim. As she watched him pull away in the car, her heart sank as she wondered what happened to the love they once shared happily together.

She turned from the window and made her way to the back kitchen door to slip out and knock on her neighbour's window to let her know she was ready. Without waiting for a response, she returned to her house to put on her coat. She made no effort to wash or comb her hair. She could only think of the night ahead as she imagined what she might find, hoping that there would be nothing and that as she peered into the pub windows she would see Jimmy sipping a pint of beer and laughing with his friend Robbie.

She only had to wait five minutes before she could hear Rosemary shouting her name as she pushed open the kitchen door. Lizzie returned with a response that she was in the sitting room. She stared at her neighbour, hoping she would not detect the terror in her voice as she said, "I'm ready just got to get my purse for the bus fair to me Mam's. I can't face the walk tonight. The bairns have kept me busy all day and I'm feeling a bit tired."

Rosemary returned her gaze and agreed with her that she did look a bit tired then she added her mother was very fortunate to have such a caring family and that she was happy to be able to assist with the babysitting.

Lizzie smiled briefly as a sweeping feeling of guilt passed through her. "Well then, I'll be off," she replied as she made her way out of the house. She took a final look up the stairs and shouted to her children she would not be long and to be good for Mrs Black. There was a muffled reply from the children as they carried on playing in their make-believe world of grown ups.

Lizzie made a brisk walk to the bus stop and waited for the next one to arrive. The autumn nights were turning cold and she began to step alternately from foot to foot to keep her blood flowing. She was glad that there was no one else at the bus stop; she had enough of explaining her actions for one day.

Soon the bus arrived with the conductor hanging out of the door, holding onto the rail to see if any one was waiting at the stop.

"Hello, lass," he smiled as Lizzie stepped onto the platform. "A bit cold tonight, isn't it?"

Lizzie nodded back at him with a smile. Usually she had plenty of witty remarks at the ready, but tonight her mind was on other things. She made her way to the front of the bus so that she could sit next to a window. The conductor manoeuvred his way along the aisle to collect her bus fare. Town Hall, she stated as she handed him her money. He clipped out a ticket from his machine and checked the money Lizzie handed to him.

He nodded his head as he turned back to ring the bell

for the next stop and let the fat lady in front of him shuffle along to the platform. He watched her turn her large frame sideways, lowering her stubby leg into the gutter, carefully pulling the rest of her large frame off the bus. He shook his head, wondering how anyone got in that state, then he looked around, hoping no one noticed his disapproval.

Lizzie looked out at the streets as the bus carried on into the town. It was not long before she could see the Town Hall in the distance and she knew that she would have to face her demons.

She stood up and, without thinking, took a deep breath as she walked deliberately along the isle behind the punters out for their Friday night out on the town.

The conductor smiled at her and said, "Watch what you're doing, lass," but again Lizzie had no time for small talk and kept her eyes straight ahead, fixing them on the Britannia pub in front of her.

There was a small crowd outside who Lizzie presumed were waiting for the rest of their company. She made her way towards them and pretended to do the same. She was aware they had not taken any notice of her, which was a relief as she began peeping into the pub each time the door opened. She was unable to make out anyone and decided she would have to walk through the bar lounge if she was to find Jimmy.

With one deep sigh, she pushed open the heavy glass door and stepped into the unknown.

Her heart was heavy and her eyes seemed to well with

tears as her eyes darted around the crowded room. It seemed forever but within seconds she spotted that familiar shape of her husband, sipping from the pint of beer in his hand. He was smiling knowingly at the blonde beside him who had her hand placed firmly over his thigh which she moved a slight inch in either direction as he spoke.

Robbie was opposite with another blonde hanging onto his every word, which was only interrupted by a silly giggle, which irritated her immediately.

Lizzie froze for a moment, not knowing what she would do next. She was in a trance as she moved towards the man she had loved with all her heart, the man she shared her bed with, the man she had given two children and had cared for with selfless admiration.

She stood at the edge of the table, picked up his pint of beer and poured it over his head.

The silence in the pub was only interrupted by the abuse Jimmy now spilled out at his wife. She turned and began to push the crowds away from her path to the exit. Jimmy was right behind her, only catching her by the arm as they got outside into the main street. Lizzie turned to punch him in the face but he caught her wrist and twisted her to the ground. Within seconds, the police were on hand to break up the disturbance.

Jimmy took charge and calmed it all down with a bland explanation to which Lizzie nodded in agreement so that she could get away from this embarrassing situation. When the policeman was satisfied that the brawl was over, he told them to kiss and make up.

Lizzie glared at Jimmy who was making light of the situation. She looked at the policeman and asked, "Can I go now?"

The policeman smiled, feeling pleased that he had done his job. "Yes, lass, and let your fella drink his beer in future."

Lizzie crossed the road to make her way to the bus stop.

Jimmy was left wondering whether to return to the pub looking wet and smelling of beer or return to his car, pick up Lizzie and face the music. He did not have to consider this for long as he watched Lizzie stepping onto the bus home.

Robbie and the two blondes came outside to find out what to do next. Jimmy grumbled that the night was ruined and that he would have to change his clothes before he could do anything. Robbie chuckled, asking if he wanted to meet up with them at Patsy's flat. Jimmy looked at Patsy's cute shape and thought of what might have been. He looked at Robbie, irritated by his sense of humour. "It's alright for you!" He paused then muttered, "I'll see what happens when I get home."

With this last remark, Jimmy turned away from them. He couldn't be bothered to speak to the girls. He had been humiliated and his temper was rising. The adam's apple in his neck was plunging forward from his neck, his blood pressure rising… he was going home.

Lizzie had walked to the back of the bus to sit out of the way of anyone she may have to talk to. She was numb inside, all her feelings gone. She was totally deflated, sitting with her head facing the window. She was interrupted only by the conductor's loud voice asking, "You're miles away, hinnie. Where you off to?"

Lizzie turned her head up towards the smiling, round, sweaty face in front of her. She mumbled her stop, hoping she would not have to repeat the words that took such an effort to come out of her mouth. The conductor seemed to get the message she was in no mood to talk to him, so he clipped out a ticket, took her money and handed her some small change. Lizzie's head moved slowly towards the window again. She leaned to one side and put the change into her pocket. She sighed again and could now feel tears welling in her eyes. She swallowed and lifted her head, trying to compose herself once again to concentrate on looking out of the window at nothing.

When she returned home, she knew she would have to be an actress again and not let her neighbour know the truth. She pushed open the back door leading into the kitchen where she found her neighbour putting on the kettle.

Rosemary turned, startled. "Oh, you're back soon. I didn't expect you for another hour. Would you like me to make you some tea?"

Lizzie tried to think quickly how she could get rid of the kindly neighbour. "Well, to tell you the truth, Rosemary, me Dad was managing fine and our Dorothy had got her into bed when I got there. Never mind, me Mam was grateful for the company. I don't want any tea, thank you. Just had one. You get yourself home to that man of yours."

Lizzie finally paused for breath. Rosemary looked back at her neighbour, thinking how pale and tired she looked. "Alright, pet," she said. "I can see you're tired. I'll be off then. I'm afraid I haven't put the children to bed yet. They're upstairs. You might want to bath the little one, he's been in the garden."

Lizzie nodded at her and with that Rosemary was at the back door saying her goodbyes.

Mary came downstairs with her little brother, Daniel. She'd heard her mother's voice and was excited to tell her mother about the little kitten they had found crying in the garden. Lizzie smiled, knowing the kitten would have to be drowned in a bucket of water with a brick on top of it. There were too many strays roaming around the estate, scavenging for scraps of food. Lizzie smiled at her children, telling them its mammy would be looking for it and that it would be gone in the morning.

She quickly changed the subject and told them it was bath time. She looked at Mary, thinking she did not look too bad. "You just put your pyjamas on, Mary, and we'll wash your hands and face. But you, young man," she added, "we'll have to bath you."

"No," he cried and ran out into the kitchen.

Lizzie took no notice and followed him to the kitchen sink where she filled a large bowl with water from the kettle, which she boiled a couple of times to fill up the bowl. She told Mary to go upstairs and get a towel to dry them both on. Then she carefully carried the heavy bowl of hot water into her sitting room and placed it on top of the cracket in front of the fire. She was pleased Rosemary had put some more coal on the fire, which was just beginning to burn through with a nice warm glow.

Lizzie sat to the side of the fireplace, her mind now slightly distracted from her children as the pit of her stomach felt the panic of the evening. She could feel her shoulders tighten and her hands felt pins and needles in them. Little Daniel came towards her as he felt the warm water with his little hand. Mary placed the towel down beside the bath and Lizzie picked it up, carefully placing it in front of the fire to warm. The atmosphere became calm, the only sound the background radio music Rosemary had been listening to.

Jimmy pulled his car up in front of the house. His nostrils flared as he looked into the window of the sitting room. He slammed the car door shut. He marched up to the door of the back kitchen and stormed into the house, stopping sharply as he realised his children were still up. The pause was long enough for him to gather his thoughts to plan his attack on Lizzie. His pace was slow and deliberate as he took off his jacket. He walked straight past the domestic scene to the bedroom where he threw his jacket into the wash basket. Then he sat on the end of the bed and removed his shiny black shoes and socks and then turned to pick up his old trousers from the back of the wooden chair. Next, he dumped his suit trousers in the wash basket, his deliberate movements gave way to the irrational thoughts dwelling within him.

He had no concern for Lizzie's feelings or that he was wrong to be found with another woman. Jimmy had been shown up in front of his friends and someone had to pay.

Chapter 12

Jimmy made his way down the stairs to find Lizzie helping Mary into her pyjamas. She began to undress Daniel, who was now excited about getting into the warm bath of water. She smiled as she lifted his chubby body into the bowl and talked to him about the poor mammy cat who would be looking in the garden for her baby kitten.

Jimmy sat in the armchair opposite her and glared at the scene he felt so trapped in.

"What was that all about?" he said, his voice low but the tone intimidating.

Lizzie's terror began to take over. She looked at him and asked how long he had been seeing that whore.

"That was no whore," Jimmy retorted, "but I'm looking at one now. Who the hell do you think you are, following me? What are you playing at?" His voice was loud and clear now as he watched Mary put her arm around her mother's neck for comfort.

The little girl didn't cry, the children were now used to the outbursts of their parents. The children's eyes were fixed on their father, wondering what he would do next.

Jimmy hurled abuse at Lizzie, much of which she had heard before. She felt humiliated, inadequate and unable to defend her actions. She was so brainwashed by his venom.

She picked up Daniel from the bowl of water and began to dry him. She responded by calling Jimmy a whoremaster who should leave her and let her look after her children herself, give her some peace away from him.

Jimmy glared at her. "How dare you tell me to leave the house, my house," he shouted. He stood up now and towered over her, sitting in the armchair, finishing off dressing her son.

As the rage took over him again, he picked up the large bowl of water and threw it over her. "Don't tell me to go," he yelled. "You go. Go on, you go. Get out, you bastard of an excuse for a woman!"

Lizzie burst into floods of tears as the water soaked through her tired body. She pushed past the children who were stunned for a moment as they heard their mother's screams as she ran up the stairs. Within minutes, she was running back down, having thrown her wet clothes on the floor of the bedroom, to put on the first dress to hand and an old thick cardigan which was on the bed, which she desperately tried to pull on in the panic to leave the house.

Mary stood between the front door and her mother. "Where are you going?" the gentle voice of the child enquired.

Lizzie calmed slightly to compose her voice enough to tell her daughter she was going out.

"Can I come?" Mary pleaded as her sad eyes begged her not to go.

Lizzie did not answer as she ran out of the house with only the clothes she stood up in.

Mary screamed after her, "Don't go, mam, don't go."

Lizzie had no idea what she was going to do as she walked, almost running, to the end of the street. She had no choice except to walk back along the old familiar road to Mam's house.

She walked briskly, not knowing what to expect when she arrived. She did not notice the chill in the air, or that some folk may have noticed she was not wearing a coat. Lizzie had no thoughts. She was stunned that she had left her home and her children. But she knew one thing... she was not going back.

As she reached the old familiar streets of her childhood, she stopped at the end of the lane and thought briefly of what explanation she could offer. Should she lie? But they would see through that. Anyway, what could she say except the truth.

Lizzie lifted the latch from the back gate and walked into the yard across the short stretch to the kitchen door. She lifted the latch and shouted, "Anyone home?"

She thought she heard Dad's grunt of acknowledgement which was quickly followed by Mam's voice. "In here, hen. What's up? It's a bit late for you to visit?"

Mam took one look at her daughter's face and no more was needed to be said. Mam sat down and Lizzie followed. "Well, lass, what happened this time? I told you, you should have never married that Catholic. He's no good. What happened, lass?"

Lizzie lifted her head slowly and looked at her Mam. "I've walked out for good this time and I've left the bairns with him."

Her Mam's eyebrows lowered as she looked at her rebellious daughter. "You know, lass, there's no room here for any more bairns. I've got Dorothy and young Jack, I can't take on any more."

Lizzie nodded her head. "Aye, Mam. I know but can I stay for a while until I get me old job back and get on me feet?"

Mam did not speak at first. She nodded at her daughter then glanced over at Dorothy, who at this point read her thoughts and put in, "There's no problem sharing the room, Mam. I get on with our Lizzie and she is family."

Mam looked back at Lizzie. "Well, that's settled then. Have you brought any clothes with you?" She knew her daughter had come to her door with what she stood up in but asked anyway.

Dorothy again added that they were the same size and she could borrow anything she wanted until she got on her feet. Lizzie smiled, thanking them, and as she got to her feet, she said she was too tired to talk tonight. "Do you mind if I have an early night, Mam? I've got too much on my mind."

Mam nodded in agreement. "You get yourself a good night's sleep. I'll see you in the morning."

Lizzie left them both with puzzled looks on their faces and made her up way upstairs to bed. She changed into Dorothy's borrowed nightdress and as she lay inside the bedcovers, she began to look back on her life, wondering how it had all gone so wrong.

The next morning, Lizzie opened her eyes to find that Dorothy had already left for work. She could hear no sounds from Jack and presumed he must have left for school. She got out of bed, feeling stiffness in her neck and back which she hoped would go as she stretched her arms up over her head.

She noticed Dorothy's dressing gown on the back of the bedroom door and without thinking she was tying the cord around her waist. She made her way downstairs, rubbing her sore eyes as she thought over the tears she had shed and the ones she had had to fight back.

She slowly opened the sitting room door to find Mam reading the Gazette in her armchair. Mam glanced over the top of her glasses. Acknowledging her daughter, she smiled at Lizzie and said, "Sit yourself down and I'll make a cuppa."

Lizzie nestled into the cosy armchair and stared into the blazing fire. Mam was soon handing her a cup of tea and Dad went on reading his paper.

Mam sipped from her cup and waited for her daughter to signal that she was ready to talk.

Lizzie sipped away until eventually she announced, "I've left them. I've left him and me bairns. And I'm not going back." With that final statement, she burst into tears again.

Dad carefully placed his newspaper on his lap and looked over to the chair Mam was sitting on. Mam raised her left eyebrow to indicate to Dad he wasn't needed.

Dad then announced, "Aye, then I'm off to the allotment." He stretched himself out of his armchair, patted Lizzie on the head, pressed his lips tightly together and left the room, shaking his head from side to side.

Lizzie poured her heart out to her mother. Mam nodded and gave a smug reply that she had been warned not to marry that posh bastard.

"If I could get me hands on him now, I'd chop his balls off." Mam never did mince her words.

Lizzie felt comforted by them. But now came the final blow.

"You know, hen, me and your Dad are happy for you to come back, but there's no room for them bairns. If you leave him, you'll have to leave them."

Lizzie thought for a moment as she stared at her Mam's unemotional face. She'd known that there would be no turning back. She nodded and sniffed then picked up the corner of her sister's dressing gown, wiped her eyes and then her nose as if to compose herself in agreement with her mother's decision on the subject.

Lizzie had gone full circle back to the house she grew up in.

As the days passed, Lizzie settled down but she soon realised if she was to move back into her parents' home, she would have to get a job and earn some money to support herself. She decided she would make her way down to Moores Stores to ask for her old job back. She was well experienced in shop work and hoped they needed counter girls. She had a good wash at the sink when Mam had finished with the breakfast plates.

"I'm going to the store today, Mam," Lizzie said, "to see if I can get me job back."

Mam smiled, happy that her daughter had settled with them. "I'm pleased to hear that, lass." Mam paused for a moment as she wondered if Lizzie was missing her children, then she decided to keep quiet, safe in the knowledge Lizzie was a strong-minded girl, a grown women who was well capable of making up her own mind.

Jimmy was finding life difficult. He had taken time off work to care for his children, but after a full week had gone by with no sign of Lizzie, he knew he would have to make some contact with her. She would be at her mother's, he thought to himself, and the prospect of knocking on that door brought shivers to his spine. Something would have to be done quickly; his savings were going down as he counted his money in the shoebox he kept hidden under the floorboard in the bedroom. On top of this situation, his daughter Mary had taken ill again with her asthma and Daniel had begun wetting the bed.

He looked worried as he watched his daughter struggling for breath, lying propped up on the couch in front of the fire. As he looked at her face, he noticed how red and swollen it was becoming. He tried to make her drink hot milk with an egg beaten up into it which he hoped would give her some strength. Mary sipped at the warm drink but immediately began to vomit into his lap. Jimmy was becoming anxious. He had never seen her as bad as this and felt unable to cope. He reassured his daughter there was nothing to worry about and that he would change his trousers. He returned to her with a moistened cold cloth, to try and get her temperature down, but as he wiped her head, she began coughing again and as she leaned over to be sick into the bucket Jimmy was shocked to see blood circulating in the water at the bottom. He jumped up and told his daughter he would just pop out to ask their neighbour to come in and take a look at her. A feeling of panic took over him as he tried to explain to the kindly Rosemary how worried he was about his daughter.

Rosemary wiped her hands across her pinny and nodded to Jimmy, indicating she was following him. She walked behind him as he made his way into the sitting room.

Jimmy sat down alongside his daughter and carefully placed his strong hands between her tiny armpits to pull her forward. Rosemary watched as the limp body of the child was turned so that her skinny legs dangled over the side of the couch. As she coughed again, unable to muster enough strength to take a deep breath, Rosemary suggested he get the doctor immediately.

"I'll go to the phone box for you. I know the number. You have the same doctor as me. Derwood, isn't it?"

"Yes," Jimmy said as he cradled the child slumped into his chest.

It was not too long before Rosemary returned, breathlessly telling Jimmy that the emergency doctor was on his way. Jimmy nodded to her, his face anxious at the thought he was unable to do anything except wait. Rosemary tried to smile but felt it was quite inappropriate as she looked with pity at a man who was clearly not used to the task of looking after a sick child.

She wanted to ask where Lizzie was, but as she had heard the many rows through the thin walls that joined their two houses together, she decided that Lizzie must have finally left. She took a deep breath and said, "Well then..." She paused. "I'll be off, me husband will be wondering where I've been. I didn't tell him where I was going when I left the house!" She smiled, but there was no response from Jimmy. He continued to look down at Mary as she slept in his arms.

Jimmy was woken from dozing by the doctor's gentle nudge on his shoulder. He opened his eyes and tried to remove himself from his sleeping daughter.

The doctor took charge now, asking what had happened and adding, "Take your time."

Jimmy apologised as he explained the symptoms of his daughter to the doctor who was nodding while he opened his black leather bag.

Jimmy gave a sigh of relief as he completed his

description of Mary's illness. He then told the doctor he would just nip upstairs to check his son was still asleep and he left the room.

When he returned, the doctor turned slowly to Jimmy and asked where the child's mother was. Jimmy explained they had rowed but that he was expecting her back quite soon. The doctor pushed the centre of his glasses so that they settled at the top of his nose. "Well, your child is gravely ill. She has asthma, as you know, but she also has measles and I feel she should have her mother with her at this time. I am fearful for her and the next few days will be crucial in her recovery. I don't feel it necessary to admit her to hospital tonight. However, I will call again in the morning and make my decision then. I will leave you with these tablets. See if you can get her to take one every four hours."

Jimmy nodded as he thanked the doctor for coming out so quickly. The doctor reassured him, stating that you could never be too careful with children. He said there was a mini epidemic of measles in the area and that the spots would appear in with the next day.

Jimmy decided to leave Mary downstairs and that he would sleep on the chair. He'd had no idea she had measles, he thought to himself as he turned to leave the room and check on Daniel. He climbed the stairs slowly, trying to decide his next step. He paused for a moment and then decided he would have to ask his mother to come and look after his children. He hated the thought of going to his parents, but he was now desperate to get back to work.

He was deep in his thoughts as he looked at his son, sound asleep, unaware of the problems around his family. Jimmy thought about lying to his parents, perhaps he could tell them Lizzie was caring for her own mother for a short time, but he shook his head and finally slumped onto the end of the bed. He took a deep breath as he leaned forward, resting his head between the palms of his hands. He felt totally helpless for the first time in his life.

Chapter 13

The following day Jimmy decided he would ask Rosemary to sit with the children while he drove across the town to ask his mother to look after them so that he could return to work. He'd decided he would pretend Lizzie was caring for her mother; this, he thought, would give him some time to think. He decided he would have no option but to contact Lizzie and ask her to return to the family home.

Rosemary smiled at Jimmy. She was glad to hear he was going to enlist some help. She had not slept easy in her bed, wondering about Jimmy and the children she had grown so fond of. Jimmy explained to her that the doctor would be calling to check on Mary. His voice sounded easy. His daughter had slept through the night and she could sit up on the couch today, he explained, smiling as he pulled on his jacket.

"I won't be long. I'm sure my mother will be pleased to help out."

Rosemary returned his smile and told him not to worry.

Jimmy's heart sank as he walked deliberately from his car to knock on the door of his parent's upstairs three roomed flat. His father opened the door, his head moving slightly backwards from his neck as he wondered why his son was paying them a visit.

"Not at work?" his father asked as Jimmy squeezed passed him in the lobby way.

"No, dad. Lizzie's at her mother's and I need some help looking after the bairns."

His father nodded as he followed his son's footsteps up the steep staircase into the sitting room at the top of the landing. He looked at his mother, sitting darning socks in front of the black range fire. The kettle was on the fire boiling and he could smell some pastry cooking from inside the oven of the range.

"Smells nice, mam," Jimmy smiled, hoping the lies he was about to tell would go unnoticed by his observant mother.

"Scones," she replied. "You're just in time for a cuppa. What's up? Don't usually see you much these days."

"Well, I'm at work, mam, you know that and I've got the bairns!"

She turned towards him with her knowing look, staring directly at him. She uttered no words but Jimmy knew that she knew he did not have a lot of time for anyone but himself.

He sat down on the couch directly in front of the fire. He looked at his mother as she got up from the armchair on his right hand side. Her silver grey hair was brushed back away from her gentle face, and her large square shaped body covered his view of the fire as she leaned forward to pour the water from the kettle into the brown earthenware teapot. His father settled into the armchair to the left side of Jimmy and smiled contentedly to see his son spending a little time with them.

Jimmy turned towards him, not quite knowing what to talk about. He glanced his father up and down and noticed how well he was looking, his tall lean frame and clear skin giving no signs of age. Jimmy thought the only give away was his bald head, which was framed only by silver hair growing sparsely at the bottom half of his skull.

"Scones smell good, dad," said Jimmy, who found it difficult to make small talk with his father. His father smiled as he got up to help his wife with the tea.

Jimmy's mother gave the pot to her husband, telling him to pop it onto the table and to get the cups and plates out of the sideboard. Soon the table was set and the small family group settled down to buttering the scones and enjoy a cup of freshly made tea.

Jimmy settled back into the couch and approached the subject he had come to see them about. "I've got a bit of a problem, mam. Lizzie is looking after her mother and I need a bit of help with the bairn…"

His mother stared at him. He's lying, she thought to herself, and asked, "How long for?"

Jimmy replied, thinking he was making progress. "I'm not sure, but if you could come and stay until things are sorted…"

Before he could go on any further, his mother put in, "Jimmy, her mother has a daughter living in the house. I know she works but there is also the father in the house." She paused. "Now how about coming out with it?"

His father gulped his tea while watching them and waiting for his son to reply.

Jimmy knew better than to continue hedging around the subject. "Well, mam…" He took a deep breath. "Lizzie has left me and the bairns."

His mother stared at him for a moment and then took a sip from her cup. "We'll come to the house tomorrow morning, but you better make sure you get her there too. I want to speak to the two of you together."

Not another word was spoken. The small family meeting was over. Jimmy left his parents' flat and got into his car. He drove to his friend's house and decided to ask him for assistance in approaching Lizzie. As he knocked on the door of Robbie's terraced flat, he hoped he was home. Slowly the door opened to Robbie's head peering from behind it. He looks rough, thought Jimmy, as he looked at the thick tousled hair and big blue eyes half closed from the deep sleep he had been woken from.

"What's up, Jimmy? I'm on night shift you know! What you doing here at this time of the day? I thought you had the bairns to look after."

Jimmy ignored his tiredness as he entered the flat. He began to tell him the whole story, ignoring the tired look of his friend.

"I need your help," was Jimmy's final remark, "and I need you to come to her mother's and knock on the door and ask her to meet me. I can't. As soon as her mother sees me, that'll be it."

Robbie tried hard to look interested in his friend's problems but sleep was trying to take over his body.

Jimmy then announced, "Come on, get your clothes on and we'll go now. Me mother insists on seeing her at the house tomorrow so there's no time to waste."

Robbie grudgingly got up from the armchair he had settled in and made his way into the bedroom to get some clothes on. He took a deep breath and sighed as he looked at the unmade bed he wanted to crawl back in to. He passed Jimmy to go into the kitchen. He knew his friend would not give him time for a cuppa so he turned on the cold tap and cupped some water in the palms of his hands and threw it into his tired face.

Jimmy was becoming impatient as he stood up to hurry his friend along. "Come on, I want to get this sorted out as quickly as possible."

Robbie ignored his remark and indicated he was ready by picking up his jacket which had been lying on the back of a chair.

Jimmy led the way to his car without speaking a word until they arrived at the corner of Gerald Street. Robbie got out and walked to the front door of Lizzie's mother's house. As he knocked, he noticed that Lizzie was already looking out of the window. She must have noticed him walking down the long garden path. He smiled at her and she nodded at him from the window. Robbie turned away from the door; he was feeling slightly uncomfortable at the task ahead.

Lizzie opened the door without speaking, so Robbie took the lead. "Jimmy's on the corner. He wants you to come home tomorrow to talk things over. He wants you back, Lizzie. Will you come?"

Lizzie looked back at Robbie without any emotion showing. "Yes, I'll come. Tell him I'll be there at one o'clock."

Robbie nodded and smiled back at Lizzie as she closed the front door. All Robbie could think of as he rubbed his watery eyes was getting back into bed.

"She'll meet you at one o'clock," said Robbie as he sat back in the car.

"Good. Thanks, my old friend." Jimmy started the engine of his car ready to take Robbie home again.

Jimmy returned to his own home to be greeted by Rosemary.

"The doctor's been," she announced with a smile. "He said she's a lot better and that he would not admit her to hospital. However, she needs constant care. Is Lizzie coming back?"

Jimmy smiled, relieved his daughter was improving. "She's coming tomorrow. I hope we can sort things out then."

Rosemary said no more as she patted Jimmy on the shoulder. She passed by him to make her way across the path that joined their homes together.

The next morning Jimmy got up early. He was woken at five by Mary's coughing and gasping for breath. He was very attentive to her needs and carefully propped her up in her bed and told her he would make a cup of tea for them both. She smiled and nodded to her dad who she loved just for being him. After they both finished their tea, Mary relaxed back into her pillow and Jimmy waited until she fell asleep before he left the room to go downstairs to set the fire away.

He soon had the sitting room warm from the blazing fire. He cleaned all the hearth and fireplace and then began the household chores to give a good impression to his parents. He felt confident Lizzie would return. Surely she would rather be with her children and him than living back at home with her parents. Jimmy began to cook breakfast. He loved a good fry up and took the opportunity to do this while his children were still asleep. He could always think better on a full stomach.

Lizzie had thought long and hard about this moment. She would make demands on Jimmy if he wanted her back to look after him and his children. He would have to mend his ways and his womanising would have to stop. The only way she could see that happening was if they spent more time together as a family and she limited the time he spent with Robbie. She was careful not to let her Mam know too much about her day off to meet Jimmy to discuss their future together. Mam was aware of the change in her daughter as she spent time getting ready in front of the mirror.

"Got something nice planned for your day off, hen?" Mam enquired.

Lizzie knew better than to lie. "I'm meeting Jimmy. We're going to talk things over."

Mam stared for a moment. She knew her daughter would make up her own mind. "Well, you know how I feel about that, Lizzie. You have a home here if you need it."

Lizzie was pleased to hear that her mother was keeping her own counsel. She smiled at Mam as she pressed her lips tightly together to press the lipstick she had applied into its place. She took one last look in the mirror, wet her second finger with her tongue and carefully ran the finger over her eyebrow to smooth out the short hairs.

Mam turned away; she could not resist shaking her head as she walked into the kitchen to put the kettle on the stove. She knew her daughter was making a big mistake.

Jimmy looked around the room and was pleased with his efforts. He now had the children settled, with Daniel playing happily on his bicycle in the garden. He had carried Mary downstairs and settled her on the couch with a blanket over her in front of the fire. She looked very red from the measles and she was struggling for breath but Jimmy thought her strength was improving and, with her mother back to care for her, she would get better quickly. He was keen to get back to work and earn some money.

He had avoided the rent collector for the last two weeks and his savings were getting low.

He looked at the kitchen clock hanging on the wall and knew his parents would be turning up any minute. He filled the kettle to boil for a pot of tea and took out some custard creams from the packet he had bought from the corner shop. As he began to prepare a tray, he heard a quiet knock on the back door and immediately shouted, "Come on in, it's open."

His parents squeezed through the back door, passing the collection of household items which were collecting in the lobby way and restricting the entrance. His father smiled broadly, while his mother's face showed no emotion as she nodded to her son.

"I've just put the kettle on. Go and sit yourselves down in the sitting room. Mary's asleep on the couch, but don't worry, she's sound."

Jimmy felt uncomfortable as he placed cups and saucers on the tray he had ready with the custard creams. He warmed the teapot with boiled water and then popped some tea leaves into the pot to brew with boiled water. He carefully carried the prepared tray into the sitting room and placed it on the corner of the dining table. His mother got up now to lend a hand. She placed the tea strainer over the first cup before the tea was poured on top of the milk at the bottom of the cup, and handed the first cup to his father with a biscuit placed on the saucer and continued until three of them settled with their cups and saucers placed firmly on their knees.

There seemed an uncomfortable silence, which Jimmy felt compelled to break. "Thanks for coming, I really appreciate it."

But, before Jimmy could continue, his mother interrupted. "Is she coming back then?"

His father lowered his head to watch into the cup of his tea, while his mother continued, "Don't think for one moment we can look after your children at our age!"

Jimmy nodded to them both. "Well, I'm hoping you can help me to persuade Lizzie to come back."

His mother's look changed. "Persuade a mother to come back to her children!" She shook her head unable to comprehend the statement her son had just made.

His father put in now, trying to calm the situation, "Well, let's just wait for Lizzie and see if we can get this sorted out."

They both nodded to him and picked up their cups to drink their tea.

Lizzie sat quietly on the bus that would take her to the Simonside Council Estate. She began to go over in her mind all the demands she would make on Jimmy if he wanted her back with him and the children. She would tell him that the boy's nights out were to end and that they would spend time together as a family. He must now be fed up looking after them on his own, so she felt sure he would listen.

She sat in the bus, trying to get comfortable on the ridged back of the bus seats and as she looked out the window, she recognised her stop coming into view. She got up from her seat, straightening her clothes as she made her way down the aisle. The bus conductor smiled, which she returned and as she stepped down, supporting herself on the rail, she heard the ring on the bell as the bus pulled away from her. She took a deep breath as she stepped down from the curb to cross the road and make her way through the two streets until she reached Sydney Gardens. She felt her stomach turn as she prepared her thoughts towards meeting Jimmy, telling herself not to waver from her demands and that this time she had to stick to her guns.

As Lizzie approached the house, she noticed that there were visitors sitting around the fireplace. She stopped for a moment to work out who the figures were. As she stared into the window, she felt her blood run cold, realising that Jimmy's parents were sitting with him. It would be impossible for her to make her demands on their marriage. She took another deep breath and, feeling her temper rise, she marched down the path, pushing open the back door leading into the kitchen. She heard the mutters of conversation coming from the sitting room and within seconds Jimmy was in the kitchen to greet her.

"Hello, pet. How are you? I'm glad you made it okay. Daniel's in the garden and young Mary's ill again. Go through and see her. I think she should wake up soon." Jimmy finally stopped for breath and smiled at Lizzie, hoping she would return his gesture.

Lizzie scowled at him and asked under her breath, "What are they doing here?"

Jimmy replied sheepishly and in a whisper, "They are helping me out, pet." He hoped this would satisfy her curiosity but seeing her facial expression he knew this was not the case.

Lizzie ignored his comments and pushed past him into the sitting room.

Jimmy's parents both looked at her, not knowing how to handle the situation, but Jimmy came into the room behind Lizzie and said, "Sit yourself down next to the bairn. She's always asking for you."

Lizzie bent over Mary and stroked her hair away from her forehead. This was enough to waken the little girl from the light sleep she was in.

"Mam," she mustered from her sleep.

"Hello, pet. How are you?" Lizzie asked the question but she was not interested in the reply. She was furious that Jimmy had allowed his parents to be there when they were to discuss their future together. She continued to smooth out Mary's hair.

Jimmy's mother put into the conversation now. "The bairn's got measless and her asthma's back. She needs her mother and Jimmy can't have any more time off work. It's about time you both got your differences sorted out. These bairns are more important than you two!"

For the few seconds that followed, Jimmy's father stared into his teacup and Jimmy cringed as he knew the statement, although factual, would only fuel Lizzie's temper.

Lizzie felt the blood rise in her neck and as she pulled herself up from the crouched position she was in, she turned on his mother. Lizzie leaned over the elderly woman sitting self-righteously perched on the chair and pointed her finger in between the old woman's eyes.

"You look after them," she shouted at her.

The silence in the room was only broken by Lizzie turning towards Mary, telling her it would be alright as she gently pushed her daughter's hair off her face again. Lizzie lifted her head high and left the house as quickly as she had entered.

Jimmy moved towards Mary and held her hand. "It will be alright," he said, repeating Lizzie's statement as he looked into her eyes for any sign of upset. Mary only nodded and smiled; she was too weak to make any effort of protest. He turned to his mother.

"Now what, mother?" he asked.

His mother paused trying to collect her composure. "Well, you can't look after them on your own and we can't be coming back and forward up here every day. You will just have to move in with us."

Chapter 14

Jimmy stared as he thought of them all in the three-roomed upstairs flat.

His father raised his weary body, as he thought of his grandchildren in his tiny rented flat. He picked up the cups and placed them on the tray to carry them into the kitchen. As he placed the tray at the side of the kitchen sink, he shook his head and thought to himself how pointless it was for him to make any comments or protest. He knew that anything he had to say would fall on deaf ears.

Jimmy sat glued to his seat. He watched as his elderly parents pulled on their coats to leave his house. Only his mother's voice saying, "We'll be off then!" roused him from his thoughts. He pulled himself up from the chair to see them out of the front door. As he turned to join his daughter again, he felt totally lost. How could he take his children to that tiny flat in Laygate to live with his parents?

He stood for a moment, looking down at his daughter trying to smile at him while her heaving chest tried to breathe. This brought Jimmy down to earth with a bump, and his anger rose, wondering what sort of woman walked out on her children. He lost no time in telling Mary what was happening and as he made his way to the garden to bring Daniel into the house, he began by telling him that his mother had left him and that they were going to live with Nana and Granddad.

Daniel started to cry. He did not understand what his dad was saying but his voice held such fury that he was terrified. Mary did not move. She showed no emotion; all she knew was that her dad would look after them.

Jimmy immediately stormed upstairs and began to pack all their clothes into two shabby brown suitcases that had broken locks on them. He took two belts and strapped up the cases, forcing down the clothes. He struggled downstairs, carrying them into the tiny passageway at the bottom. He paused, looking around for the moment, wondering how he would pack up his goods to move the family into his parents' flat.

It took three days to move all their belongings to the flat. Jimmy purchased tea-chests and borrowed a van from the bus depot to transport them in. His mother gave him the front bedroom and told Jimmy to move the double wardrobe forward at one side; this meant that he could stack all their goods behind it in the alcove. He brought the cot for Daniel even though he had outgrown it months earlier. There was not enough room for anything bigger. Jimmy would have to share the double bed with Mary and no doubt Daniel, he thought to himself as he looked at the cot pushed into the only available space in the far corner of the room.

Jimmy's parents looked gravely on as their home was taken over by their son and his children. Mary was now approaching seventy years of age and her husband, although in good health, was sixty-five. At this time of their life they did not expect to have to be taking care of a young family. Jimmy turned and looked sadly at his parents. He thanked them, saying how much he appreciated them taking him in and that he hoped it would not be too long before he got a place of his own. However, in reality, this was not to be.

After the trauma of leaving her home and children, Lizzie had no alternative but to return home to her parents. Her stubborn nature struggled with the resulting situation she had now found herself in. She sat quietly on the bus, looking out of the window, watching folk go about their daily business and felt a strange feeling of emptiness. She was now alone without her children. She had hoped Jimmy would come around to her way of thinking and make a fresh start. She still loved Jimmy and wanted to keep the family together but she felt she was justified in her actions and now he would have to suffer to bring his children up on his own. She sat quietly muttering to herself, "He won't manage and I know he won't put them in a home... he'll soon be crawling back."

When Lizzie got off the bus, she walked slowly along the railway track and through the back lanes until she reached her parents' house. Mam was standing at the back door talking to her neighbour after hanging out her washing on the line that stretched across the lane and was nailed to the wall opposite. Lizzie looked at her mother's thin but strong square shaped body, wrapped tightly in a full length, washed out pinny, covering a cream coloured blouse with the sleeves rolled up to her elbow. The remains of a brown coloured skirt hung slightly below the pinny where her thin legs revealed thick nylons with tiny folds appearing as they came down to her chequered slippers with red pom-poms on the top.

As Mam gossiped, she caught sight of her daughter, which prompted her to cut short her conversation, as she did not wish her neighbour to quiz her daughter about her current state of affairs. She immediately stood away from the door and stated, "There's our Lizzie. I better get the kettle on," and with that last remark, she turned and left her neighbour with her mouth open ready to ask questions. After being denied this opportunity, she quickly turned to Lizzie to ask her how she was.

Lizzie knew all too well her Mam wanted to avoid gossip until she knew exactly what the situation was. Lizzie nodded to her neighbour. "I'm fine. Ready for a cuppa with me Mam," she smiled wryly. Then added, making a final comment as she passed through the back door. "You alright, then?"

Her neighbour smiled briefly, knowing she was being told to mind her own business.

Lizzie stopped at her Mam's side, watching her pour the hot water into the teapot.

"All sorted, hen?" her Mam asked without looking at her daughter.

"No, Mam. It looks as though I might be living here for awhile, if that's okay with you and me Dad?"

Mam didn't look around and carried on getting the cups out of the cupboard. "Well, pet, that's up to you. There's always a spare bed for you." She felt a sadness sweep over her, knowing how her daughter had wanted to make a fresh start with Jimmy. She also knew how stubborn she was.

Lizzie sat down on a kitchen chair to sip slowly at the hot tea, and no further words passed between mother and daughter.

Jimmy found life with his living with his parents very difficult and spent as much time as possible working away from home. His parents' view on young children was that they should be seen and not heard, a saying young Mary did not understand until she became a teenager. The daily routine soon established itself and the children soon began to know their place in the small flat and became quite withdrawn.

However, Jimmy's mother loved her grandchildren and thrived with them around and the responsibility that came with it. She was given a purpose in life once more.

On Mary's first day at school, she was taken on the trolley bus from Laygate up to Stanhope Road where they disembarked to walk to St Peter and Paul's Catholic School.

Mary joined with the Easter intake on a bitterly cold day. She felt very lonely as she let go of her grandmother's hand to be led into a huge classroom filled with a noise level she had never heard before. Children were crying with little comfort being offered to them, while the others ran riot around the adults before they left. There seemed to be nothing else for her to do but to sit down on one of the little red chairs at the end of a red table. No one took any notice of her as she looked around at the chaos, until eventually she heard a loud guttural voice calling out from the door of the classroom, "Quiet please."

Suddenly there was a deathly silence. Even the crying stopped while the only adult left in the classroom walked forward to stand in front of a blackboard and easel. The voice continued to boom and terrify all the children into continued silence. "Now then," the voice continued, "I want none of that crying now that you have started school. From now on, you will do as you are told by your teacher. I'm your teacher and my name is Miss McManermy and I have one or two rules you must know about. The first rule is you must never be late in my class and you must always bring a handkerchief. If there's one thing I can't stand, it's sniffing in the classroom. Now every morning when I tell you to take out your handkerchiefs you will all blow your noses. The next thing — and the most important — you don't speak until I tell you and you must put up your hand like this." She lifted her arm and pointed her hand towards the ceiling then said, "I don't want you waving it about. You just put your arm up like this and if I want you to speak, I will tell you. If I don't, I will ignore you and you will put your arm down without speaking."

The children stared back at Miss McManermy, terrified to open their mouths for the rest of the day. Miss McManermy then went to sit at a large desk facing the children. She opened a large book and told the children that this was her register and when they heard their name being called out, they had to say as loud as they could, "Yes, Miss."

For the months that followed, the children soon learned the routine of the register, the handkerchief and one thing which Miss McManermy forgot to tell them about on that first day, which was that all girls had to tie their hair up away from their shoulders. Either in ponytails, bunches, buns or plaits. On the one occasion when Barbara Connelly's rubber band snapped, Miss McManermy's voice could be heard booming from her classroom, shouting for one of the older girls to find a band and tidy that girl up immediately. From that day, all the girls remembered to keep spare elastic bands and ribbons in their satchels.

When Daniel became old enough for school, things had changed a little, with the new infants teacher sending for older brothers and sisters to join their siblings to give them moral support on their first day. Mary sat holding Daniel's hand until they were told to leave the room when all the crying had stopped and the kindly Mrs Bainbridge asked if they would all like to come to her desk and take a sweet from the large brown paper bag lying open on her desk. Not all the children felt bold enough, but Daniel thought getting sweets from the teacher was great and he was one of the first up to the front of her desk. However, when he returned home to his grandmother that night to tell her all about his first day, she told him not to tell such 'tall stories'.

"Teachers don't give sweets to children…" She paused. "Whatever next," she muttered as Daniel was about to continue with his tall story. He looked at Mary first and decided from her face that he would drop the subject.

Much of Mary's early school days were spent in passive anticipation, trying to fit into the mould. It was much the same at home with her grandparents as she quietly played with her brother under the dining room table with their tiddlywinks or snakes and ladders.

Life in the tiny flat was a routine that never changed over the next three years. Bath night was always Sunday, when the tin bath was dragged up the back stairs from the washhouse and placed behind the couch and slowly filled from kettles of boiled water. Privacy was the hope that no one looked over the top of the couch! The children had a routine of meals at the table when they came in from school, then they could play out in the back lane when they had finished and cleared the dishes away. If they were off school, they had to help with the chores around the house. Mary liked Mondays where she could watch her grandmother in the washhouse, boiling up the water for the washtub and rubbing the clothes against the poss tub to remove the dirt. Her grandmother allowed her to pick out the clothes with wooden tongs then she would try to lift them up to the wringer. This was always difficult as they stuck together and were quite often too heavy for her little fingers. Her grandmother always smiled and told her she could help turn the handle on the wringer, much to Mary's delight.

Every Sunday they were taken to mass and soon there would be great excitement, as Mary got ready for her first communion. There was a lot of preparation at school as the children read about the life of Christ and how they would soon be very privileged to receive his holy body in the form of unleavened bread. They were told they would have to fast from the night before but on the day of the first communion they would be having a special breakfast at the school afterwards.

There was much excitement from the girls who took great delight in talking about the dresses that they would be wearing. Mary knew her grandmother would be making her dress and that she already had the white satin material and new bobbin of thread sitting over a pattern ready to be cut out from the tracing paper. Jimmy's mother spent hours making the dress perfect along with the carefully made veil, which she edged with a layer of lace to place on top of her granddaughter's head. Mary stood patiently as the braded plaits were pulled into place on top of her head so that the clips from the veil could keep everything in place.

Daniel was allowed some porridge before church on

the special day but Mary, like her grandmother, would be fasting. Her grandfather would have a fry up ready for his wife on her return. Sunday was his day to help in the house and by the time they returned from church each week, he would have all the vegetables prepared, waiting in pans of salted water. The meat would be roasting in the oven and the Yorkshire pudding mix would be standing in a bowl on the windowsill. Although Sundays were always a boring days to the children, the wonderful smells of cooking and Sunday's dinner remained with them throughout their lives.

One day while Mary was waiting outside the infant's school for Daniel, she noticed a familiar figure walking towards her. She froze as the lady called out her name and asked if she was waiting for Daniel. Mary nodded to the lady who then called out, "I'm your mam, Mary, I'm your mam!" and she put out her arms to hug her.

Chapter 15

Mary, unsure how to react, did not move and looked up into the lady's eyes.

"I'm going to come home with you on the bus," the lady announced, "and I want you to ask your dad if I can see you every week."

Daniel was joining them now and looking just as bewildered as the lady took hold of each of their little hands to walk along the street with them. As they got onto the bus, Lizzie asked her children lots of questions about school, their friends and what they did after school. The children answered each of her questions as the bus rocked along the trolley tracks.

Daniel was the first to ask a question "Do you know where my Nana lives?"

Lizzie smiled pleased she was making some progress.

"Yes, of course I do."

Mary wondered why she had not been before.

"I want you to ask your Nana when I can take you out. We can go to the pictures, or the beach."

Daniel again piped up, "I've been to the beach with Nana and Granddad."

Lizzie again smiled, glad to hearing him communicating with her. She looked lovingly at her daughter now, who sat looking out of the bus window, seemingly unaware of the conversation she was having with Daniel.

When the bus reached the stop for Laygate, the children got up and looked at their mother.

"It's our stop," Daniel said. "Are you coming to see Nana?"

Lizzie took a deep breath, thinking of the best way to approach her mother-in-law about taking the children out. "Yes, I know. Go on you two, I'll follow you."

The children scrambled past her and Lizzie watched them along the aisle as the bus conductor pulled the cord to stop the bus along the tracks. Lizzie smiled at him as she followed the children off the bus and along the street until they came to the beginning of Taylor Street.

"We usually go down the back lane," said Mary to her mother. "Do you want to knock at the front door?"

Daniel stared at them both, waiting to be told which way to go home.

Lizzie thought for a moment and then said, "You two go home as normal, round the back. And tell your Nana I'm at the front door and want a word with her."

Mary nodded back to answer her and took hold of Daniel's hand to pull him along to the back lane. Daniel would normally have pulled his hand away from his sister, not wanting anyone to think he was a baby. But this time he let himself be led along, his head turning to watch his mother until she was out of sight, and the trio walked parallel lines until they reached number 174.

Lizzie walked as slowly as she could to give the children time to get up the back stairs and ask the question.

As the children made their way along the lane, Daniel pulled away from Mary and began to run.

"Wait for me," Mary shouted and she took off running along behind him.

Daniel was first to reach up for the latch at the back gate and ran up the yard as Mary closed it behind them both. He climbed the two stone steps and opened the door leading into a steep dark stairway. They both clambered up the stairs to try and be the first to ask the question but in chorus they echoed, "Our mam is at the front door. She wants to speak to you."

Their faces beamed with pleasure knowing that their mother was going to ask to take them out. The silver-haired lady looked lovingly at them as she wiped her hands on her pinny and put her arms behind her back to unfasten the string material that kept it together. She did not answer them, only told them that tea was on the table. The children went into the sitting room where Granddad was reading his paper at the table. He told them to wash their hands in the scullery and to come back and sit down quietly at the table.

Jimmy's mother took hold of the banister as she went down the front staircase, wondering what on earth Lizzie could want after all this time. She opened the door and stared at the young woman who was still married to her son but no one had seen for a year.

Lizzie went straight to the point. "I want to see my

children again and I want to take them out every week on my day off." She watched her mother-in-law's face, waiting and hoping for a positive reply.

Jimmy's mother felt her blood run cold as she looked at the woman who had left her children to God and good neighbours. "You know how our Jimmy feels about that. We've talked about this and he doesn't want them to see you. You left them, now get on with it." And with that she turned and closed the door in Lizzie's face.

Lizzie stood motionless, looking at the brown painted door. She could not cry but felt a lump in her throat get bigger and bigger until she thought her cheeks would burst they were so full of blood. She dragged her opened hand over her face and rested them on her throat trying to compose herself before she turned around to face the world. She knew it was no good. She knew Jimmy would be paying her back for as long as it took. She knew she had no one to turn to and she knew she had nowhere to take her children to live with her.

She took a deep breath again, held her head high and turned to walk back up the street to the bus stop. She resisted looking back down the street knowing that the old woman would be watching from behind the curtain. She told herself that she would get by; she had to until the day she would be with them again.

Jimmy's mother struggled up the stairway, her body becoming too heavy for the stairs that faced her with every chore she had to perform. She was becoming weary looking after her grandchildren, but she thought to herself, what else can I do? She opened the door to the sitting room and watched as the children questioned her with their eyes.

"No, you two are not going out with your mother. It's up to your dad to decide about that. Not me. Now come on with you, get your tea eaten. I haven't been slaving over that hot stove all day for nothing."

The children looked at each other briefly and then put their heads down, pushing the knife and fork into the mince and dumplings.

Finally, the day came for young Mary to make her first Holy Communion. She knew she had to fast the night before and was not allowed any breakfast that morning as she watched Daniel eagerly eating his porridge with a wry smile on his face, hoping that his sister was very hungry. He could not see what all the fuss was about but felt that he was missing out on something special.

Jimmy's mother hurried her granddaughter along, telling her it was time to get washed and ready in time to catch the bus to church. They would carry her communion dress and veil in the small, brown travelling case, which was only used on a special journey. Little Mary would get dressed and ready in the church hall.

Daniel finished his breakfast and got himself ready without any fuss and waited for them by sitting himself at the top of the stairs.

Their Granddad smiled. He had been through all this before many years ago with his own children.

"Well, I'll be off, Granddad." Jimmy's mother smiled at her husband, using the pet name everyone called him by.

The children hurried down the stairs as fast as they could, opened the front door and waited for their Nana to join them.

When they arrived at the church hall after the short walk from the bus stop, Jimmy's mother felt quite tired, but when she entered the hall her face lit up, looking around her at all the children. The girls wore a variety of styled dresses but all were gleaming white satin and lace and the veils framed their angel-like faces with a beauty only an innocent child can portray. She helped Mary with her dress by standing in front of her to allow some privacy even a young child expects, and when the dress was finally tied with a sash, making a huge bow at the back, she began to plait Mary's hair to place the veil firmly with grips on the top of her head.

She stood back and smiled at her work. She'd loved every minute and hour she had spent putting together this little creation.

Daniel wandered around the room, looking at the boys wearing white shirts and bright red ties. He watched as the teachers fussed around, smudging a little brylcream on the top of any head if someone's hair looked untamed. One fat lady even had black boot polish at the ready to make sure that even the poorest of boys looked their best on the big day.

Soon a bell was rung and everyone knew it was time for the parents to leave and make their way into the church before the children. Jimmy's mother took hold of Daniel's hand and pulled him along with the crowd.

The church was warm that day and the sun shone through the stained glass windows. Candles burned brightly and the scent of fresh flowers filled the church. A faint smell of incense was always present but today scented blooms were dominant from the donations made from the little sisters of the church. Jimmy's mother and Daniel managed to get a seat next to the aisle, which meant they would easily see all the children as they passed.

A silence could now be heard as the children approached the front of the church to kneel down and form a line of white angels, waiting for the priest to descend down from the alter, for them to receive the body of Christ.

The rehearsals went according to plan with all children receiving their small circle of unleavened bread. When the last boy left the altar with a smile that would melt your heart, the rest of the congregation stood up to take their place and receive the body of Christ that their faith had taught them. The one and a half-hour ceremony was over in no time, everyone was so excited and happy to be taking part in this very special day. As the congregation stood up to make their way out of the church, some stopped in the foyer to admire and purchase rosary beads, statues and prayer books that had been neatly placed on a small table top stand. This was indeed a very special day.

Jimmy's mother waited outside patiently for her granddaughter to finish her specially prepared breakfast, which all children received in the school hall after making their first Holy Communion. Daniel was feeling left out and kept pulling at her coat to ask when they could go home.

"Soon," she assured him as she tried to stretch to see above the crowd in front of her.

"Look, Nana," cried Daniel. "I can see her." He was peering between two big-bellied ladies having a conversation; his head was just underneath the bellies and he could see his big sister clearly. "Mary," he shouted and left hold of his grandmother's hand to run towards her.

They both smiled and skipped towards the plump elderly lady who cared for them. Jimmy's mother smiled proudly as she guided them away from the school. "Come on now, your Granddad will be waiting for us."

Daniel skipped ahead of them, leaving Mary to take hold of her Nana's hand until they got home to their flat in Taylor Street.

Life continued in a set routine for three years until one Monday morning Jimmy's mother took a fall down the back stairs as she was carrying a basket of dirty washing to the wash house to start the first chore of the week.

Granddad heard the fall and raced down the stairs to

her aid. "I'm alright," she retorted, hating the feeling of helplessness.

"You're not! Now careful as I get you up."

The old woman knew she was beaten and accepted his help. This was a turning point and they both knew life was getting the better of them. It was time to take things easy.

That morning they worked together in the washhouse at the bottom of the yard. Boiling water and possing clothes in the tub, until finally using the tongs to put them through the wringer. One good thing, she thought to herself, and that was that Jimmy was taking his shirts to the Chinese laundry at the end of the street. At least she never had to worry about washing and ironing them. Jimmy was too fussy by far; nothing would be good enough for him to wear unless it was perfect.

Granddad stretched the line across the yard, wiped it with a damp cloth and together they hung out the week's washing. Jimmy's mother decided she would take the bed linen to the Chinese laundry tomorrow when she felt a little stronger.

That day they quietly discussed the prospect of approaching their son to improve their situation by moving to a larger place and getting some help around the house. They both acknowledged the commitment to the children, however something had to change.

Jimmy's mother finally said, "We'll speak to him tonight." Decision made. "Now you let me do the talking," she added with determination, knowing how easily he was swayed by another point of view.

Granddad nodded back at her at the same time, opening the Gazette to see what was going on in the world.

That afternoon Jimmy's mother busied herself preparing the vegetables for the evening meal. She felt her thoughts passing through her brain as she began deciding how she would approach her son that evening. The small scullery did not lend itself to two people and she carried on quietly on her own, only stopping once or twice to fill the kettle with water to take through the living room and place on top of the burning coals from the black range fire to brew a pot of tea.

"It won't be long before the children are in from school. Will you have your dinner with them or wait for Jimmy?" she asked her husband without seeing his face behind the Gazette.

"Just as you like." he commented.

She nodded and decided they would eat together and she would keep a plate hot for Jimmy. She needed her meal to digest and she wanted to be in control tonight to discuss the future with her son. So as the evening closed, the two elderly grandparents waited for their son to return.

That night Jimmy was due home from Coventry. He had been away for four days on his normal bus route. He had now become friendly with another landlady, which suited him.

"No ties," he kept telling his friend Robbie, who was now having an affair with a barmaid that was becoming very demanding on his time. "You'll never learn, will you? You could have the best of both worlds if you played your cards right!" he insisted.

Robbie just turned his head to the side and smiled. He was happy with his lot and never looked further than the day in hand. It must have been his upbringing in Ireland, Jimmy thought to himself, where he had to fish in the river to put his share of food on the table from the age of nine. Jimmy knew it was useless and smiled back.

By the time Jimmy got the bus parked up in the cleaning bay for the next morning's shift, he was exhausted. He picked up his jacket and bag from behind the driving seat and wearily descended the steps from the bus. Wiping the sweat from his brow, he walked slowly walked towards his Morris Minor. Jimmy was not prepared for the night that lay ahead of him. He looked around and said goodnight to couple of the drivers as he got into the car to get himself off home. He pulled out the choke and began to turn the engine over, thinking only of the piping hot dinner that he knew would be waiting for him. He waved to the two bus cleaners as they passed by him to start the night shift, sweeping up the rubbish left behind by the travellers.

Jimmy smiled to himself, happy to get back to the routine of home life with his children.

However, tonight was different. He felt the deathly quiet atmosphere as he climbed the staircase of the flat. When he reached the top, he opened the first door on the landing and looked inside for a moment to check on his sleeping children. He nodded to himself as he stepped backwards to quietly shut the door of their bedroom so that he did not disturb them from their sleep.

He heard his mother's voice saying there was a chill in the air and she would close the heavy winter curtains for the night. As soon as he opened the door of the sitting room, he instinctively knew that something was not quite right. He ignored his feelings and placed his bag of washing behind the couch and carried on into the scullery to wash up before his dinner.

"Dinner smells good," he remarked as he leaned forward to get the cloth to take his plate out of the oven. He then sat down at the dining table behind the couch to eat his dinner and read the Daily Mirror he had bought that day.

His mother sat quietly waiting for him to finish his meal, and then she got up to pour out some tea from the pot.

"We'd like to have a word with you before you go to bed, Jimmy."

Jimmy lifted his head, pushing his glasses further onto his nose as he asked, "Nothing up with the bairns, is there?"

"No, nothing like that but it does involve them."

Jimmy took a deep breath, not realising he was sighing at the same time. He rose from his chair, folding the paper and placing it on the wooden dining chair behind him. He moved towards the couch and sat down, wanting to relax but his body was sitting upright, waiting to hear what they had to say.

His mother took charge while keeping her eyes focused on her husband to indicate to him to keep his mouth shut. "We've been talking, me and your dad and, well, we're getting on now and the children are growing up fast, and… well, we're finding it a bit hard. I'm seventy four now and your dad's not getting any younger. We're crowded in here and with you being away all the time…" Mary paused as she watched Jimmy's face drain of its colour. He had never once given a thought that his parents would not be able to cope or that he might never get back with Lizzie.

Jimmy slowly tried to gather his thoughts and finally asked his parents what they wanted him to do.

"Well," his mother piped up again, "if you don't want the bairns to go into a home…" She paused as the shock on Jimmy's face took its toll, and she quickly added, "We don't want them to but we need a bigger place and either you find a job where you can come home every night and get us some help in the house, or you will have to get their mother back."

Chapter 16

Jimmy could not speak. He stared at them in disbelief until he finally gathered his thoughts and answered, "Well, if that's what you want, I'll look around tomorrow for a bigger place to rent and I'll ask at work to be home every night. It will be less money but maybe I can take on another job to make the money up at weekends."

His mother smiled, nodding her head as she did, her husband making no comment as he continued puffing away on his pipe.

Jimmy rose wearily from the couch to go to bed. He made no further comments as the night came to an abrupt close. He changed into his striped pyjamas and sat on the side of the bed. Suddenly the tears he felt dripping from his face turned into sobs, which woke his daughter.

Mary rose from her sleep to put her tiny arms around her him. "What's the matter, dad? Why are you crying?"

Jimmy made no effort to disguise his grief. He could not move as he let the tears continue to fall. What a mess he was in. How did this happen, he began to question of himself.

Mary didn't move either and kept her arm around her father until the tears stopped and he told her to go back to sleep. She got back under the warm covers to carry out his wishes and slept.

The following morning, Jimmy got up early to prepare breakfast for everyone and take the children to school. A ride in the car was great excitement for them as they packed their satchels with a reading book. When Jimmy dropped them off, he went straight to the paper shop to see if any flats or houses were being advertised. He had two days off work and had to find a bigger place for the family as quickly as he could.

As he sat in the car, his finger slowly following the lines of adverts, he came across an end-terraced house in Alfred Street. It had three bedrooms and a kitchen, which advertised a 'bath'.

That sounded exactly what he was looking for, he thought as he started the engine to make his way into the town to view the property.

As he pulled up outside the red door, he considered that it looked quite tidy and hoped the inside would be the same. He opened the car door and smiled at a passer-by who said, "Nice morning."

Jimmy smiled. "Hope it's here for the day," he replied, looking up the clear sky. He took four steps toward the front door and knocked, looking around the wide street as he did. It had a workingman's club across the road, and he wondered if it was noisy at night, but his thoughts were interrupted when an elderly lady answered the door.

"I've come about renting the house. Is it still available?" he asked, smiling.

The lady smiled back at Jimmy and invited him in, turning her wide frame to point along the passage. "I've just put it in the paper, and you're the first enquiry I've had. I'll show you around."

The first room on the left was a parlour that looked as though it never got used. A piano was the first item of furniture to greet them as she opened the door.

"I'll be leaving the piano as I won't be having any use for it. I'm going to live with my daughter and it's too big to take."

Jimmy smiled; he knew his mother always wanted a piano. The lady then led him into a cosy living room where the fire was burning brightly. "I live in here most of the time," she remarked. "The kitchen is through that door; go ahead, I'll follow you."

Jimmy's eye followed the outline of the room. It had a large Formica larder cupboard to the left, the back door which led into the back yard, facing him.

A few items of washing were pegged on the line to dry which led his eye towards the outside toilet where the door was open at the bottom of the yard. He turned to smile at the lady.

"Don't mind me," she remarked. "Go ahead and have a look around."

Jimmy moved towards a sink, which had a cupboard below, as the lady continued with her comments.

"It's a gas cooker... quite new," she added looking

past the sink, "and as you can see the bath is just behind you."

Jimmy turned, looking at the bath that was hidden underneath a huge bench.

"Plenty of work space," she said. "Well, if you would like to look upstairs at the bedrooms, follow me."

Jimmy was very satisfied as he followed the lady back into the passageway where the steep staircase led to two doors facing each other at the top.

They entered the first room, which was light, airy, and led into a smaller room.

"Nice if you have young children," she remarked as she watched Jimmy's face smiling at her. She led him back towards the third room, which also had another door. "That's the attic. It never gets used so it's not decorated or anything."

Jimmy opened the door where he stared at a dark dirty staircase which had words scratched into the brown walls. He slowly climbed the steep dark stairway leading to two dark attic rooms; the wall had etchings and various names scratched into the surface. Jimmy nodded to himself as he made his way back down, and smiled at the lady as he came back into the bedroom, "This is just what I'm looking for. Do you require rent in advance?" Jimmy reached into his back pocket to feel for his wallet.

The lady answered, "A month is what I'm looking for and I can be out by Friday."

He pulled out the pound notes from his wallet and asked if he could have a receipt.

"Of course," she answered. "Come downstairs. You will want a few shillings change."

When the transaction was complete, they shook hands and the kindly lady showed him along the passage to let him out. Jimmy left the house feeling elated that he could return to his mother with good news that he hoped would keep the family together.

On his return, she accepted his news with limited excitement as she now wondered if she would be able to manage to look after a larger house. "Will you be able to sort out some sort of help?" she asked.

"Mother," Jimmy shouted as his nerves reached breaking point. "One thing at a time. I have to see work tomorrow about changing my hours. Now look, you will just have to wait until we move. There is a lot to do if we want to be in by next Friday. I think I'll be able to borrow a works van to move our stuff, so let's just concentrate on that."

His mother nodded as she felt her life being pushed along. She felt sorry for her son who she knew was doing his best, but at her time of life, a young family was taking its toll.

The next few days were hectic as everyone packed up all their belongings to move into the town. Jimmy managed to change his hours at work so that he could help and be home every night. He had no time to think about himself as he tried desperately to keep everyone happy.

"Are we going back to live with our mam?" asked little Mary who was old enough to remember her.

"No," Jimmy said. "Your mother left you both. She will not be coming back."

Mary made no response and turned to play with her dressing dolls, changing the paper dress of the doll, and pressing down the paper tag over the shoulder of the cardboard figure.

As the week progressed, the house was gradually packed up and the family left the two bedrooms flat to move into number 6 Alfred Street. The children loved their bedroom, which was large enough to play in without knocking into the furniture. Jimmy's mother liked the kitchen and was happy to have a bath, although the fire had to burn all day to heat the water. It was easier than boiling pans of water to fill a tin bath, she thought.

Family life settled into a routine, with the children starting St Bede's Catholic School opposite Derby Street Baths. Daniel settled into the infants and made friends easily with his carefree nature. Their grandparents were doing their best to meet the demands of a young family, but slowly, even in the bigger house, they became tired with the situation they found themselves.

Even now that Jimmy was coming home every night to help in putting the children to bed they were beginning to feel their age.

School life for young Mary was another daunting change. She became a loner, and was unsure of whom she could trust, finding it difficult to make new friends. One night when she walked home alone from school, she was followed by two of her classmates.

"How does your mam like it without you"? they taunted her.

Mary began to shake inside; she did not turn around to answer them and began to quicken her step to try and hurry on ahead. The girls behind giggled and continued to badger her. Mary felt her eyes well up but she dared not turn her head to let them know how hurt she was. As the voices stopped, Mary realised that they had taken the turning into the back lane of Elizabeth Street, leaving her to compose herself in the silence of her lonely walk home.

The months went by with no extra help that had been promised by Jimmy. This led his mother to ask to talk to her son about the situation. Jimmy finally told her to approach the council to ask for an old person's bungalow.

"They are building along the John Reid Road," he announced. "See if you can get one." He thought that would be the end of her pleas, giving him more time to work things out.

His mother got up early the following morning to take the bus to the Town Hall to put her name on the council list. She sat patiently in the waiting room for an hour. Finally, a bespectacled man who was looking down at the paperwork in his hand called her name. She nervously struggled out of her seat to follow him into a room where he invited her to sit down. She took her time in explaining the domestic situation of her son, and how tired and old she felt caring for a young family now that she was in her late seventies. The bespectacled man kept nodding his head and reassured her that he would do everything he could to help. Jimmy's mother felt elated when she left the corporation offices. She was sure that her prayers would be answered.

It took nine months before the confirmation of a bungalow dropped through the letterbox. She took a deep breath as she prepared to tell Jimmy that he would now have to find someone else to care for his children. Once again, she waited until he had finished his evening meal and the children were settled in bed.

"Jimmy, you had better sit down," she said. "I have something to tell you."

Jimmy sat in the armchair next to the fire waiting to hear what his mother had to say.

She continued, "We have heard from the corporation and they have confirmed that a bungalow is ready for us to occupy next month."

The shock on Jimmy's face said it all. His mother did not attempt to offer any support and added, "You will have to find someone to care for the children, and maybe you could try the priest? He might be able to recommend a lady from the church who might wish to make some extra money."

Jimmy continued to stare at her, but now he added a

gentle nod to his head. He was unable to argue or persuade them to stay, and he knew that it was too much for them both. He finally said, "I'll go and see the priest on my day off." He rose from the chair and without another word left the room to go to bed. This time he shed no tears. He had to face up to his responsibilities and sort out his life with the children.

Two days later Jimmy found himself sitting in the priest's house being given a cup of tea by the housekeeper. She seemed a kindly woman; maybe she would do the job, he thought to himself. Jimmy looked around the cosy sitting room, admiring how clean and polished everything was. The walls were covered with holy pictures where the light flickering from the fire made them come alive with bright colours. His thoughts were interrupted by the sound of a man's voice as the solid wood door at the other end of the room was closed. The voice had a melody to it with an Irish accent stronger than his friend Robbie's had.

"Good day to you, good sir. How can I help?"

Jimmy immediately rose from his comfortable armchair to shake the priest's hand. He thanked the priest for seeing him at such short notice.

"Sit down," the priest interrupted and sat in the armchair opposite. "Would you like another cup of tea?" he asked as the housekeeper brought in a tray laid with a china teapot, cups and saucers.

Jimmy nodded and handed the housekeeper his empty cup to top up with tea and milk. "Thank you, Father" he said and smiled at the housekeeper as she completed the task.

The two men settled back, taking a sip of tea while the housekeeper handed them a plate of biscuits. The two men resisted the biscuits and Jimmy began to tell the priest about the dilemma he found himself in.

After Jimmy took the priest through his life story, leaving out the affairs, lies and situations he preferred to forget, he finally asked the priest if he could assist in finding him a suitable housekeeper to look after him and his children so that he could continue to work and keep his children with him as a family.

The priest nodded, looking soulfully at Jimmy, making him feel that he would have the solution. It took some time before he spoke which made Jimmy feel he was coming to a conclusion and was about to give him a woman's name to contact. Jimmy sat quietly for some moments looking at the priest in anticipation.

"Well," the priest announced eventually, "this is a very difficult situation. I have listened to all that you have had to say and I can tell you that I feel the best solution…"

Jimmy stared, waiting.

"…is that you contact your wife and ask her if she would be willing to take you back for the sake of the children. It is now four years since she has had contact with them and you are telling me that she has not married again. Maybe she still loves you? Maybe she is hoping that this day would come. My advice to you is to contact her… if she dismisses your proposal, come back and see me. But I have a feeling that this woman will be missing her children after all this time. Take my advice and ask her."

Jimmy stared in disbelief at the words that this Irish priest had muttered. However he had no choice but to carry out the instructions. His mother would be pleased at this, he thought to himself as he stood up to shake the priest's hand. However these final words were the last that he wanted to hear.

As he drove the short journey back home, he was deep in thought, wondering how he could make contact with Lizzie again. He felt unable to ask Robbie and he knew it would be impossible to use his parents. His heart hung heavy as he opened the front door. Even the homely smell of cooking could not lift his spirits.

His mother smiled broadly at him, anticipating good news. "Well, did the priest have someone in mind?" she asked as she put the dinners on the table.

Jimmy shook his head, not wanting to discuss the matter in front of the children.

"The children know, I've told them," announced his mother.

Jimmy was furious, knowing his mother's tactics in getting something done this time. His back was up against the wall and as he looked at his children, the idea came to him.

"Mary…" He crouched down at the table so that his eyes were level with his daughter's. "The priest has said I should contact your mam and ask her to come back to live with us." He watched Mary's frail face break into a smile. "But I will need your help."

Mary put her fork down to wait for her dad to tell her how she could help.

He continued, "I am going to drive to the shop where your mam works. I want you to go inside and ask her to come out to meet me."

Mary nodded at him. The conversation stopped, Jimmy sat down, his mother put a plate of dinner in front of him and the family finished their meal.

Chapter 17

The next day Jimmy told Mary he would meet her from school and that they would go together to see her mam. He waited patiently outside until she came out and got into the car. "We'll drop Daniel off with Nana and then we can go up to the shop," Jimmy announced as he turned over the engine.

Within fifteen minutes, they were parked at the back of the shop, a little way along the lane. Mary got out of the car to do as she had been told. She felt happy as she entered the shop to see if she could spot her mother.

Lizzie was stunned to see her daughter walk into the shop as she was wrapping up some butter.

"Hello, pet. Have you come to see me?" asked Lizzie as she looked over to Mary. "I won't be a minute." She quickly took payment for the butter, put the money in the till and came from behind the counter to take Mary's hand and ask her why she had come.

Mary explained that her dad was outside and wanted to see her. Lizzie's heart skipped a beat as she looked around at her workmates to see if anyone had heard. No one appeared to take that much notice so Lizzie called to them both that she would be nipping out for a moment. She smiled gently at her daughter as she followed her footsteps out of the shop into the back lane. Her heart fluttered as she saw the back of Jimmy's head in the driver seat of the car.

Mary opened the car door which made Jimmy jump soulfully from his daydreaming. He looked at Mary briefly and turned his shoulders around to see if Lizzie was behind her. Startled, he got out of the car and walked around the back to have a private word away from Mary's earshot.

"Thanks for coming out, Lizzie. I need to speak to you. Could you meet me after work? Perhaps we could call somewhere quiet for a drink?" He stared at her for a moment. He could see that she was taken aback and prompted by her silence he carried on. "I know it's short notice, I can take you home after if you are going out." He paused, hoping that this time she would speak.

She did. "I finish at half five. You can meet me here if you come back then."

Jimmy smiled, grateful for the opportunity to try and get his life back on track.

They both stood looking at each for a moment, and then Jimmy nodded his head and said, "See you then." He turned without making any further eye contact with her and returned to the car to start up the engine and drive away.

Lizzie was left almost dumbstruck as she watched the little green Mini drive out of the back lane. She took a deep breath. This was the first time she had seen him in almost four years. She had been close enough to touch her daughter. All she'd had were glimpses of her children through the schoolyard gates on her day off. Her daughter Mary was growing fast but was still frail-looking from her bouts of sickness caused by asthma.

Lizzie returned to the shop to carry on her work. She picked up the damp cloth at the end of the counter and started wiping down the shelves. No one made a comment from the back of the shop where the girls were taking a tea break and Lizzie decided to keep quiet until she found out what Jimmy had to say when they met later.

Mary sat quietly in the car, waiting for her dad to tell her what was going to happen.

Jimmy sensed her concerns and said, "I'm going to meet your mam later to see if we can work out a few things. You know your Nana's getting old now... well, maybe your mam might come back to look after you and Daniel. I'm going to ask her later."

Jimmy did not look at Mary and she continued to keep quiet, not knowing what she should say. They continued in silence until the car pulled up in Alfred Street and they got out to enter the house once again.

Jimmy nodded to his mother's expression asking him what had happened. "I'm meeting her tonight when she finishes work."

His mother nodded back as she placed plates of dinner on the table for the family to take their seats. Jimmy pulled his newspaper from the outside pocket of his jacket and sat at the table, opening it to place over the sugar bowl. He was not reading anything in particular; he only hoped that his mother would leave her remarks until he returned from speaking to Lizzie.

His mother's frustration could be felt. She wanted to tell Jimmy what to say to her and insist that she take responsibility, however on this occasion she was not given the opportunity and quietly ate her dinner with the family.

Mary and Daniel were first to finish and looked at their grandmother who told them to take their plates into the kitchen. She again looked at Jimmy, hoping for some comments but Jimmy pushed his glasses further onto his nose and looked at his watch.

"Well, I better have a quick wash before I go." He rose from his seat, careful to avoid his mother's stare as he went into the kitchen to have a quick wash of his face and hands at the sink.

His mother gathered the dinner plates to clear the table and as Jimmy came out from the kitchen, she passed him, trying to catch his eye to give him her advice.

Jimmy ignored her, preoccupied with what lay ahead of him. "I'm off now, mam. See you when I get back."

His mother grunted as she continued with her tasks. Jimmy left the house feeling very vulnerable for the first time in his life.

Lizzie could hardly contain her apprehension and excitement. Her friend Gladys asked her, "What's up? You look like you have seen a ghost."

"I have!" she said as she turned to look her friend in the eye. "Did you see Mary come into the shop earlier?"

Gladys stared and shook her head, wondering what Lizzie would have to say. There was little to tell other than she would be meeting Jimmy later to talk. Gladys showed her obvious concern for her dear friend who had shared so much of her life in the last four years since they met. All she would say to her friend was to be careful and to think of her future.

As it came to closing time, the girls filtered into the back shop to collect their coats and make their way home to continue with the household chores waiting for them. Lizzie made sure that she was last out of the shop. She did not want anyone to know her business so that they could gossip while her back was turned. She splashed her face with cold water and wet the end of her middle fingers to smooth out her eyebrows. She ran her fingers through her hair and then took her coral lipstick from her handbag to moisten her lips with colour.

Happy now with her appearance, she picked up her coat to leave the shop. She turned slightly as she approached the door to say she was leaving. "I'm off, Mrs Anderson," she called to the assistant manager who was counting the money in the till from the day's taking.

She nodded in return as she carried on counting as if Lizzie had not spoken.

Lizzie took a deep breath as she walked the few short steps into the back lane where Jimmy was waiting in the car. He quickly got out to greet her as she approached, asking where she would like to go to talk. Lizzie replied that she did not mind and got into the passenger side, lifting her flared skirt up to avoid it getting caught in the door as Jimmy closed it.

He was now taking deep breaths as he wondered where to go to put his request forward. He smiled, turning towards her as he started the engine. "How about the Golden Lion? It's on the way and it should be quiet at this time."

Lizzie agreed and they drove the short journey towards the pub.

They both felt awkward as they got out of the car to make their way into the pub. Jimmy told Lizzie to sit in the corner near the window and asked her what she would like to drink.

"I'll have a stout," she smiled and he raised his pointed finger to the barmaid, pointing to the pump he wanted the beer pulled from. Nervously, he carried the drinks across the floor towards Lizzie who immediately picked it up.

"I'm ready for this... it's been one of those days."

Jimmy felt at ease with Lizzie as he sat down to join her. "I'll come straight to the point, Lizzie. Me mam and dad are struggling with the bairns and they have got themselves a new bungalow on the John Reid Road." He watched Lizzie's puzzled face and carried on. "I was hoping that you would come back to us? I know it's been a long time but I have never wanted to marry again and I don't know if you have any plans to remarry?"

Lizzie's jaw almost dropped. The man that she had never divorced or had any contact with had now met with her after almost four years, asking her to resume her life with him as if nothing had happened.

She cleared her throat. "This is a bit of a shock. I will have to think about everything."

Jimmy put in immediately, "Yes, yes, I understand. I know I wasn't the best of husbands, but I don't go out that much now."

Lizzie considered her position quickly. "You would have to take me with you if came back."

Jimmy nodded again.

Lizzie continued. "We would have to sort out housekeeping and I would want to keep on my job," she added as if she had waited for this moment for a long time.

Jimmy was relieved to be making so much progress. "Whatever you say. I just want us all to be together again!"

Lizzie paused for a moment to take a sip from her stout. "I will have to talk to me Mam and Dad. They've been good to me all this time… it's the least I can do."

Jimmy nodded again. "Yes, I know. I know they never did like me. Most probably they'll tell you to keep away from me."

Lizzie was quick to defend herself. "It's up to me what I do."

Jimmy smiled. He knew Lizzie, and knew that Lizzie had already made up her mind to come back to him. They continued with the small talk until the drinks were finished and they were ready to leave. He drove her home, feeling happy that the situation would soon be resolved.

She chatted happily until they reached the corner of her street and she realised that she would have to break the news to her parents.

She told Jimmy to stop at the corner, just as she had done when they first met.

Jimmy smiled, knowing exactly why. "When will you let me know?" were his parting words as he leaned across the car to speak to Lizzie as she got out.

"You can meet me after work on Saturday night," she said. Then turning, she quickened up her step to face the music at home.

Lizzie took a deep breath as she opened the back door leading into the kitchen. Don't know what I'm worrying about, she thought to herself, it's my life. With that thought, she lifted her head high, greeting everyone, and wasted no time in telling all her plans.

No one spoke and they all turned to look at Mam for guidance.

"Well, you know how I feel about that man," Mam said. "You're making a big mistake, my lass. You'll live to regret it if you go back to him."

Lizzie turned to face her mother but for the first time in her life, she kept her mouth shut. She knew better.

Lizzie was so excited when Saturday came around. She arose early, packing a small bag with a change of clothing and some toiletries. It was getting near Christmas and she was hoping to spend it with her children for the first time in almost four years.

The day went quickly, with customers in and out all day, buying the weekend groceries. As usual, there was a lot of gossip in the shop. No one was ever in a hurry to get home to the daily chores; part of the pleasure of going to do the shopping was to bump into friends and neighbours.

Lizzie knew everyone and was looking forward to the day she could tell them that she was getting back with her husband and children. She anticipated it would be a shock to them after all this time. Everyone had stopped gossiping about that a long time ago so no doubt tongues would start wagging again. Lizzie did not care; she had long ago given up on what people thought.

As the shop cleared, the girls began to collect their coats and shopping bags to start the weekend and enjoy time with their families. Lizzie held back, making sure she served the last customer, giving her more time to be on her own to tidy herself up before meeting Jimmy. No one seemed to notice and she was able to have the back shop to herself to wash at the sink and change her clothes.

Mrs Anderson called from the shop while counting the money. "Going out straight from work, Lizzie? Someone's keen!"

Lizzie made small talk but was careful not to give anything away. "You know me, Mrs Anderson, hate to lose any time enjoying myself." She hoped this would satisfy her curiosity and within seconds, this was confirmed by Mrs Anderson's giggle and comment, "Wish I was single again."

Lizzie tried hard not to reply and laughed just a little to offer her some agreement.

"I'll be off now." Lizzie smiled as she made her way through the shop to leave.

Mrs Anderson called without looking up from counting the takings. "Yes pet, enjoy yourself."

Lizzie quickened up her steps, hoping no one would see her getting into Jimmy's car at the end of the lane. This time as she got into the car, Jimmy leaned across to take her hand.

"I'm glad you decided to come," he said.

Lizzie smiled nervously at his tender touch.

As they pulled away from the back lane, Jimmy asked Lizzie where she would like to go for a drink.

"The Britannia," she replied as she was ready to forget everything that had ever happened between them and start all over again.

She took a deep breath before she entered the bar of bad memories and held her head high. Time is a great healer and having her children back in her life was all that mattered.

She had always loved Jimmy. Even when she knew about the affairs, she'd blocked them out. This time would be different. They had both learned from their mistakes and it would not happen again.

Chapter 18

Jimmy felt comfortable in familiar surroundings as they both looked around for a quiet corner to sit and talk about the future. The bar was beginning to fill up but there were still plenty of window seats where Jimmy could light up his cigarette and relax with his wife again. Lizzie let him take the lead in the conversation and gradually as the alcohol relaxed them both, Lizzie got straight to the point.

"When can I see the bairns? It's near Christmas. Will your parents be out of the house by then?"

Jimmy swallowed slowly, trying to give himself time to think before he replied. "Well, my mother hasn't set the date." He turned, hoping she would understand the position he was in.

But Lizzie was in full swing now. "Jimmy, I've started buying a few presents for the children and my sisters have too. I want this Christmas to be really special and I thought I could fill a tea chest each for them full to the top with all sorts," then she added, "especially sweets!"

Jimmy felt the pressure and tried to let Lizzie down gently, knowing his parents may not have the keys to the property before Christmas. However, Lizzie was not deterred and said she could get her brother-in-law to borrow the works van and she could deliver them. "I won't have to come into the house. I'll just meet you in the back lane and you can take them in."

Her face was appealing to him and he knew he could not refuse. That being said, the happy couple relaxed and began to enjoy the company and the tunes the piano player played to the crowd. It was not long before the banter between everyone turned into a sing song as everyone got drunk.

At the end of the evening, Lizzie fell into Jimmy's arms and he told her what she wanted to hear.

"I've missed you, Lizzie," he said with the drink taking over him. "We'll start all over again and this time it'll be good for both of us." He paused. "I've learned a lot being away from you and know what I want now. It's a family." He smiled into her eyes and knew that he had won her over.

Lizzie never spoke in response. She held onto his arm for her life and planned in her mind the future they would have and the wonderful chance they were being given to start all over again.

Jimmy returned home that evening feeling as if a weight had been lifted from his shoulders. The only problem he had was to tell his mother that Lizzie wanted to deliver some Christmas presents to the children. He knew his parents would be awaiting him and as he turned the key to open the door, he could smell his dinner warming on the stove. He opened the door of the sitting room to find his parents eagerly waiting for news of the evening he had spent with Lizzie.

His father was all smiles. "Good night, lad?" he questioned but Jimmy was looking directly at his mother.

"Yes, it seems we've worked out our differences and we both want the same…" Jimmy paused, emphasising the next statement. "What's best for the children." Then he added, "Lizzie has some Christmas presents for them and she wants to bring them down."

Without any hesitation in her voice, his mother said, "Not when I'm around. That woman has not bothered to write even a note to them in four years and now she wants to deliver Christmas presents?"

Jimmy tried to calm the situation down. "Look, mam, she's only going to drop them off in the back lane next week with her brother-in-law. You won't have to speak to her or even see her for that matter. Dad and I can carry the tea chests in."

His mother shouted, "Tea chests?"

Jimmy felt himself explaining away the years apart and how he owed it to Lizzie to make a pathway to the children. "You know, mam, this whole thing was instigated by you wanting a bungalow for you and dad."

His mother muttered under her breath but she knew it was the right thing to do. She then busied herself with her son's dinner on the table and then quietly said she was off to bed. Jimmy's father patted him on the shoulder and followed her along the passage to the front room they used as their bedroom. She muttered again under her breath as she felt her husband touching her shoulder in reassurance that things were happening for the best.

Later that week after another meeting with Lizzie, Jimmy agreed for her to drop the presents off on Thursday evening before the children went to bed. He told his parents about the delivery and as they nodded to him, he decided the time was right to give the children the news.

He made a great effort to play the whole situation down, as if it was a brief interlude in all their lives and it was only a matter of time before they would all be a family again. He was careful to add how their grandparents had an old persons' bungalow and that they would visit them every week without fail. The thought of Christmas presents being delivered brought controlled excitement to them. They were never encouraged to be loud in their grandparent's household and gave nothing away when told of the return of their mother, watching their nana's face until she announced, "Well, plenty time to get used to that. Time you two were in bed! Let's be having you, up you go."

The children responded immediately to something familiar and without another word ran out of the room and up the stairs to bed. The excitement of the evening began to take over them as they laughed with delight at the thought of Christmas.

Lizzie was so excited when Tommy, her brother-in-law turned up in the works van. She had carefully filled the tea chests full to the top with all kinds of cheap toys from the market, two selection boxes and some games which she thought would be fun to play when she finally got the chance to be their mother again. Lizzie's Mam huffed and puffed as she watched her daughter struggle out of the house, carrying the tea chests with Tommy to the van. As much as she tried to keep her comments to herself, she had to give way and release the tension by muttering to her husband what a big mistake Lizzie was making.

He sharply replied, "Nothing to do with you, lass. Keep your own counsel."

Mam picked up her paper and sat opposite her husband. She did not open it. Instead, she felt for comfort in the pocket of her apron and pulled out her cigarettes. She tore off a slip of newspaper, which she rolled to light from the blazing fire. As she leaned forward so that none of the burning paper broke free onto her carpet, she muttered again, "That lass will never learn, she's too stubborn by far."

Lizzie settled into the front of the van and chatted happily to Tommy as he drove into the town.

"Thanks a lot for this, Tommy. I couldn't have managed without you." She watched his kind face smile as he changed the gear to slow the van down to turn onto the main road. Tommy made no comments as to his sister-in-law's situation, he knew better and only hoped for her happiness that a family could bring. He himself had longed for children and was pestered constantly by Alice for them both to see a doctor, but he believed nature would take its course and these things were best left alone.

"We'll be there in no time," he answered, trying to reassure her of his approval without giving any judgmental comments.

Lizzie felt the butterflies in her stomach as they turned into the back lane on the corner of Alfred Street. She looked across at the watch on Tommy's wrist and saw that they were early by five minutes.

Tommy stretched his arm across towards her and took hold of her hand. "We'll get the chests out ready," he said, knowing that her nerves would get the better of her if they sat still for too long.

Lizzie nodded in agreement, pleased that Tommy knew exactly how she was feeling.

Inside the house, Jimmy was watching the clock. He thought he heard a van pull into the lane and got up from the couch to go into the yard to check.

His father followed him. "I'll give you hand," he said, not wanting to cause any embarrassment.

Jimmy was just about to light a cigarette to calm his nerves but he put it back into the packet. "Thanks, dad," he said with relief as they went out into the darkness.

Tommy and Lizzie were just about to lift the second chest from the van when Jimmy called out, "We'll do that."

Lizzie giggled. "Don't worry about me. I can manage with Tommy, but you could take the first one in if you like."

Jimmy and his father picked up the chest and took it into the yard, Tommy and Lizzie following with the second. Tommy told Lizzie to leave it at the back gate, so embarrassingly they put it down and waited for Jimmy to come back outside. "Thanks, Lizzie. The bairns will be over the moon when they see all this."

Lizzie smiled. "See you tomorrow then."

Jimmy looked at Tommy, who had now turned to go back to the van. "I'll pick you up after you finish work. It's my day off before the weekend overtime. Let's go for a bite to eat."

Lizzie smiled answering, "See you then." Then she turned, feeling emotional as she joined Tommy for the journey home.

As the weeks went on, Christmas came and went and Jimmy helped his parents to move their belongings to the new council bungalow in the John Reid Road. Jimmy met regularly with Lizzie to build up their broken relationship. They planned a bright future together, choosing items of second-hand furniture to build a home and another try at family life for the sake of their children.

Lizzie was kept apart from her children until the grandparents moved out. There was no love lost between them and on the day Jimmy helped his parents settle into their bungalow, Lizzie wasted no time in stamping her own mark on Alfred Street.

Lizzie was very different from the grandmother who had cared for the children and this was displayed by her light-hearted exterior as she tried to build up her relationship with her children again. She found her daughter Mary quiet and reserved, which was the opposite of her own nature. Daniel started to wet the bed again, something which upset Jimmy, as the young boy had not done this since Lizzie left them. However, Lizzie was not deterred and thought it was only a matter of time before things settled down. She began by introducing the children to her sister Gracie and her newly born twins. Mary had never been within touching distance of a baby and was curious to meet her baby cousins.

They set off to walk to John Williamson Street, which was almost an hour walking distance for the three of them at Daniel's slow pace. When they arrived at the row of terraced flats, Lizzie called out her sister's name and watched as Gracie opened the front door of the upstairs flat ready to pull the twin pram up the stairs.

"I'll give you a hand, our Gracie. Hold on."

Gracie turned and screamed out in delight. "Not a minute too soon, our kid," she continued with a loud laugh.

Mary stared at them both wondering what was so funny and took hold of Daniel's hand, watching as her mother pulled the twins from the pram and wedged one on each of her hips. Gracie laughed loudly again as she struggled, heaving the pram stair by stair until she reached the top followed by her sister carrying the twins with Mary and Daniel close behind.

Gracie took a deep breath, "Why, you bugger, the stairs get steeper every day."

Again, they both laughed as Gracie continued to manoeuvre the pram across the floor of the sitting room into the bedroom they all shared.

Mary and Daniel stood motionless, looking at their mother pop the twins onto the floor. The twins continued to watch the visitors, waiting to be entertained. Lizzie responded immediately by getting down on all fours to make gurgling noises, her face almost touching theirs, which made them squeal with delight. The twins now dragged themselves up on to their knees, pulling at Lizzie's cardigan to try to stand up.

"Put one of them on my back, Gracie," Lizzie shouted to her sister as she closed the bedroom door after putting the pram away into the corner.

Gracie picked up one of the boys and straddled him over Lizzie's back. She immediately took off around the room in any space that was available. Gracie laughed loudly as she tried to balance the child on her sister's back. Mary and Daniel sat down on the couch and watched as their mother entertained the twins in turn with piggybacks. Eventually Lizzie collapsed in a heap on the floor and giggled as the twins climbed on top of her asking for more. Gracie took over then, saying, "That's enough, you two. Aunty Lizzie is tired and wants a cup of tea."

She brought the tea tray into the room and placed it on top of the dining table, which stood in front of the back window, looking out onto the yard below.

Lizzie straightened herself up and took a seat at the dining table next to Gracie. The sisters began to talk, each keeping one eye on the twins as they tried to get the attention of the new children that had come to visit them. Lizzie called out to Mary to play with them, but Mary made no movement as she had never played with babies before and was not sure what to do. Daniel sat close to his sister, giving her the occasional glance to wonder if she would tell him what to do.

Mary was now nine years old and it was beginning to occur to her that she did not know her mother or remember her playing with her and Daniel.

After they had eaten biscuits and drank cups of tea, Lizzie announced it was time to get back home for their dad's tea. "Come on, you two," she said. "I need to get some mince at the butcher's for the tea."

The children got up and pulled on their coats, Mary helping her brother to fasten the toggles on his duffle coat while Lizzie tussled once more with the twins before she quickly wrapped herself in her coat and tied the woollen headscarf under her chin.

She sniffed and turned to Gracie. "Come to mine next week for your dinners?"

Gracie smiled in agreement. "Same time next week," she said as she watched Lizzie and the children make their way down the front staircase into the street.

As they made their way to Frederick Street, Mary and Daniel wondered how many times they would have to stop to talk to everyone. It seemed to them that their mother knew everyone in South Shields and that they would never be home in time for their dad's tea.

In time, family life began to settle down for Lizzie. Jimmy seemed a changed man who was happy to come home every night after work to his dinner which was always ready on the table. Lizzie had learned long ago that this was the most important thing to get right in your marriage, dinner on the table as you heard your man walking down the passage. This was achieved by careful timing, which had to allow for the occasional delay. Lizzie would then revert to boiling a pan of water to place the dinner plate on top covered by the pan lid.

She was surprised how quiet her children were. They had learned from their grandparents to 'be seen and not heard'. They managed to entertain themselves and had friends who lived around the doors.

All in all, Lizzie was contented with her life. She had her job which fitted in with her chores at home and she could always rely on Jimmy's father to be around for the children at lunchtimes and if Jimmy wanted to take her out for a drink at the local pubs and the weekend. However, she made no effort herself to visit his parents unless it was absolutely necessary. She blamed his mother for much of her distress and decided if Jimmy's mother had not stepped in so early to take over her household, she would not have been parted from her children for so long. But she knew she was unable to keep the children from seeing them and went along with Jimmy's plan to send them up every Sunday morning after church to visit them.

"The exercise will do them good," he said as he helped Mary and Daniel clean up their pushbikes in the back yard. They were Catholics now and Lizzie never stood in the way of holy days and the practices of the Catholic faith, which had been instilled in them by their grandmother and the Catholic teachings at school.

Every Sunday after church, the children peddled from Westoe Bridges until they reached the new John Reid Road from Simonside. The bike ride would take them up to an hour and they were always ready for the tea and packets of biscuits that waited for them. When they were fully refreshed, out came the playing cards and buttons from the button tin to use for money to gamble. When they got bored with that, Nana would get out the draughts, telling Mary on the quiet to let her brother win sometimes to keep the peace.

On the other hand, Jimmy never visited Lizzie's parents and Lizzie made no attempt to change this. Jimmy would never be made welcome at her parents' home and both families knew these ties were severed four and a half years ago when she left Jimmy with the children for a new life.

It was Wednesday morning and Lizzie was planning to finish work early for a half day. She had invited Gracie and the twins around to have dinner with her at one o'clock. The children were off school for a holy day and Lizzie was keen to get home as early to get the grandfather off home so that she could enjoy her sister's company.

Lizzie loved her job at Moores Stores and since her transfer into the town, she made more friends around the streets where she lived. Jimmy's father came every day to feed the children at lunchtime when they came home. This gave him a purpose and got him away from the never-ending chores his wife had for him. He was surprised how much he missed the chatter of children, although he spent most of the time telling them to keep quiet as he was reading his paper.

It was a fine day with the sun shining brightly and Lizzie felt happy as she walked the short stretch of back lane home when she finished work. She lifted the latch on the back gate leading into the yard and called from the kitchen as she entered, "Yoo hoo."

Granddad got up from the armchair where he was quietly reading his newspaper. "Hello, Lizzie," he said. "I'll just get my coat on."

Lizzie was pleased at the response; she would have the house to herself. Not that she would have expected him to stay; he never outstayed his welcome and was always uncomfortable without his wife by his side.

She smiled at him and said, "Well then, I'll see you out," and together they walked along the passage to the front door, which Lizzie opened for him.

Granddad pulled on his cap and fastened up his scarf, which he tucked inside his old grey trench coat. He turned rather shyly and said, "I'll be here for the bairns tomorrow, Lizzie."

They nodded reassuringly at each other. Lizzie stood until he turned the corner to catch his bus home then quickly turned to go into the kitchen to prepare some dinner for her visitors.

Soon Gracie was knocking at the front door. Lizzie called to Mary to open it and it was not long before they were all sat around the table, chatting and eating the lunch Lizzie had prepared.

Suddenly there was a noise from the passage and Lizzie realised that Jimmy must have finished early. This was not good and she quickly got up from her meal to greet him. "You're home early, Jimmy. Is everything alright?"

Jimmy looked around at the chaos sitting at his table and grunted that it was a job and knock, which meant that he had been helping the mechanic in the yard. He proceeded past the group to the kitchen. Removing his overcoat, as he tried not to trip over the array of baby items lying around. He made no effort to acknowledge Gracie as Lizzie followed him, asking if he was ready to eat some dinner.

He said he was starving so Lizzie quickly dished out his dinner onto a plate, placing it onto the table. Gracie, by this time, had got the message and began to keep the children occupied by getting down on the floor and waving a few toys at them to gain their attention. Jimmy manoeuvred himself around the room to reach his dinner and before another word could be said, he opened his newspaper to place in front of the salt and pepper pots as he sat down. He turned to glance in Gracie's direction and gave her a dirty look, which Lizzie immediately picked up on.

"Your dinner alright, Jimmy?" she nervously asked.

Jimmy removed his glasses and looked at her with steely eyes. "I can't enjoy my dinner with all this noise going on."

For a moment there was a deathly silence and the atmosphere could have been cut with a knife.

Gracie was not about to stay another moment and got to her feet as quickly as she could. "I'll be off, our Lizzie," she said and she picked up the first twin to put on his coat. Then, just as quick, she had the second wrapped up tight.

Lizzie was about to burst into tears, her temper almost out of control. She followed Gracie along the passage to help her out with the children. Gracie could hardly look into her sister's eyes and commented only to say, "See ya, our kid."

Lizzie nodded in reply and slammed the door, almost racing back into the room. The children stood watching, stunned as their mother burst into a rage. Jimmy jumped from his chair and was only restrained from lashing out at Lizzie by the look on his children's faces.

Instead, he turned his anger to his plate of dinner on the table. In one sweeping action, he cupped his hand underneath the plate to hurl it across the room. The action brought Lizzie's temper to a standstill as she waited for him to make the next move. Jimmy pushed her out of his way, picking up his jacket to storm out of the house.

She looked at Mary and Daniel and told them to go outside to play so that she could get tidied up. Mary took hold of Daniel's hand and together they went into the cupboard under the stairs to put on their coats before going outside to look for some friends to play with.

Maybe Jimmy wasn't so different after all...

Chapter 19

Jimmy was very late coming home that night and there was no further conversation in the house until a letter arrived from the council a week later.

The letter was addressed to them both so Lizzie opened it immediately. She stared for a moment and then raced upstairs to wake Jimmy. "Jimmy," she squealed. "Read this letter... it's from the council."

Jimmy opened his eyes slowly to look at her outstretched hand holding a letter.

"What is it?" he asked.

"Here, read it for yourself."

Jimmy sat up and took the letter. He reached to the bedside cabinet for his glasses and began to read the official looking document. It stated that Alfred Street was to be demolished to make land available for new properties. All residents would be re-housed in the expanding council estate called Whiteleas.

Lizzie stared, smiling, waiting for Jimmy to respond.

He removed his glasses and the two of them ended their feud by hugging each other. "We'll finally have a house of our own," said Jimmy.

"And a garden," added Lizzie. "Let's get in the car and have a look around the estate."

Jimmy nodded but a cloud took over him as slowly he thought how close he would be living next to Lizzie's family.

"Alright" he said. "We'll have a look around but I'm thinking a lot of people want new houses, we may be able to get an exchange to another estate."

Lizzie didn't answer. She knew exactly what he was thinking and decided to keep her own counsel and go along for the ride.

They drove to Whiteleas and discovered the estate was to be enormous. Bulldozers could be seen digging out huge areas of soil and foundations were already done in a number of streets that had been mapped out. Lizzie felt excited at the prospect of living so close to her family again, however she knew better than to make any comments at this early stage.

"What do you think, Jimmy?"

Jimmy paused in thought and eventually answered her. "We'll advertise and see what sort of a response we get from the Gazette for an exchange." He turned to watch her response but Lizzie knew his game and told him she thought that it was a good idea, hoping at the same time that there would be little interest.

Over the next few weeks they registered their interest with the council until eventually they were told that they had been accepted and would be advised when they could take possession the keys.

Jimmy wasted no time and placed the advert in the

Gazette for the next four weeks. He was very disappointed when he received only one reply to his advert from a family living on the Brockley Whinns Estate. Jimmy felt dubious when he and Lizzie arrived at the property. He was having difficulty understanding why they wanted to move. Lizzie decided not to get out of the car as they both recognised a neighbour from the time they spent in Sydney Gardens leading up to the time of their separation.

Jimmy turned to her. "We'll have a look around but I don't think this would be for us, do you?"

Lizzie shook her head as they both got out of the car to introduce themselves to the possible exchange prospects. Polite conversation was exchanged and the kindly couple showed them around the very neat and tidy home. Jimmy and Lizzie showed little interest but told the couple they would give them consideration along with a couple that they had already seen. They all shook hands as they parted at the front door and continued to smile and wave as they pulled away in the car.

Lizzie was the first to speak. "What do think we should do?"

Jimmy answered thoughtfully and told Lizzie he thought they should check out the property in Whiteleas when they get the keys. That way they would be in a better position to make up their minds. However, in their minds they both knew it was too close to where they'd lived before they separated and too many tongues may wag behind their backs. They needed a fresh start.

Jimmy decided he would try his hand at building up his own business and as the family used paraffin heaters to take the chill off the air in the hallway and in the kitchen, he decided that he could possibly make some extra cash selling paraffin from his own van. His plan was to work when he finished his shift on the buses and any days off including weekends.

"That way if the business eventually becomes successful, who knows…" he said proudly to the children. "I want your help to deliver the cards I've had printed. They've got a pre-addressed reply on the back and it's your job to stick the stamps on for a reply. We may even go back to collect the postcards from those who don't. You will both help me every Saturday until I get my regulars."

Jimmy got himself a second-hand courier van and got the sign writers and spray painter contacts he had to do a cheap job for him and that weekend the children were enlisted to deliver two hundred and fifty cards around the Simonside Council Estate. There was great excitement as they set off on Saturday morning, each of them trying to beat the other at how quickly they could get rid of the cards.

Within a week Jimmy was receiving replies and it was not long before he was working around the clock at his new venture. However, the excitement in the family came to a halt when a policeman knocked at the front door later that week.

Lizzie called out to Jimmy as she invited the two policemen into the house, wondering what on earth could be wrong. Before she followed them she briefly glanced outside to see if anyone was in the street to witness the visitors. And with no one in sight, she quietly closed the front door and walked along the passage.

Jimmy was now standing on his feet almost to attention, confirming his name and that he was the son of Mrs Smith, 38 John Reid Road.

"I'm afraid I have some bad news for you, sir. It's your father…" He paused before carrying on on. "I'm afraid he passed away this morning and your mother is in some distress and is asking for you."

Without hesitation, Jimmy said, "I'll get my coat."

The policeman, aware of his shock, offered to take him, but Jimmy said that he had a car at the door and would make his own way.

Lizzie was left stunned and in an attempt to break the silence, she said, "Would you both like a cup of tea?"

"No, thank you, madam. We'll leave you now to sort yourselves out." And with that everyone began to walk along the passage to leave the house.

Lizzie watched in silence as Jimmy started up the engine. He did not look at her as he pulled away in a daze from the distressing news he had received, the realisation of his loss giving in to the tears which trickled down his face in despair.

When he arrived at the door of the bungalow, he was greeted by two neighbours who offered their sympathy and left him to console his mother. Her crying was perpetual as she sobbed, telling Jimmy she could not manage without him and kept asking over and over again, "What will I do?"

Jimmy could give no answers and only held onto her, saying that he would sort everything out for her and not to worry.

"What about your sister Agnes?" she sobbed.

"Mam…" He paused for a moment. "She's on the telephone, I will ring her on my way home. She'll come up from London to be with you and you will have nothing to worry about. Now come on, let me make you a fresh pot of tea and I'll stay here with you tonight. Lizzie knows what's happened and won't be expecting me home."

Over the next week, Lizzie realised she would have to give in to Jimmy and visit his mother and sister at the bungalow before the funeral, so begrudgingly she got into the car with the family and decided to keep quiet as much as possible when she arrived there. The children did not understand what a death meant and skipped over the grass laughing and pushing each other until Jimmy shouted at them, "Have some respect, will you both. Your grandfather has died."

Lizzie quickly rushed over to them, telling how sad Nana was and that they must keep quiet. She took hold of their hands, pulling them separately into the sides of her hips.

The front door was open and Jimmy went in first followed closely by Lizzie and the children. Agnes immediately rushed over to Jimmy to hug him and as she did, she glanced over the side of his shoulder to Lizzie who was standing quite motionless, waiting for the reaction to her presence. As Agnes pulled away to allow Jimmy to embrace his mother, she calmly said, "Hello Lizzie," and without any emotion, they both acknowledged each other.

The children looked up at the slight figure of their aunt while she smiled at them and finally said, "Well, you've both grown, haven't you?" And with that she turned towards Jimmy and listened again to the traumatic events of the heart attack, which came so suddenly taking her dad's life.

Lizzie sat down on the couch in front of the fire; she felt uncomfortable remembering how little time she had for her high and mighty sister-in-law from London.

Agnes had already made a large pot of tea, which was being kept warm standing with a tea cosy over the top of it in the hearth of the fireplace. She carefully poured everyone a cup and then without speaking, took the children into the small kitchen to give them some orange juice. This was quite a treat for them as most of the time they had to drink water if they were thirsty.

Dignified conversation continued until Jimmy decided that it was best to take Lizzie and the children home.

This was to be the only time Lizzie saw the old woman. She did not attend the funeral, telling Jimmy that he wouldn't dream of attending her mother's therefore why should she share in his family grief? Jimmy did not argue, knowing too well the less his family saw of her the better.

The following month, confirmation came in the post that a property was available in Turner Avenue. This time the whole family went to view the three-bedroomed end terraced house.

When they arrived, they gazed for a moment at the newly-built properties in the street. Then they all got out of Jimmy's car to view their new home. As they entered, the new paint smell, new walls, new kitchen and beautiful clean white bathroom overwhelmed them. As they made their way through the front door, the stairs leading up faced them and to the left, a door leading into the sitting room was open.

They followed each other and the children immediately ran from one end of the room to another so that they could hear the echo of their shoes as they ran. The room was light and airy as it had a picture window at each end of it.

"Look," squealed Mary, "we have a huge garden!"

Lizzie immediately went to look. "Oh Jimmy, come and see this."

Jimmy strolled to look out of the window.

"Have you got the back door key, Jimmy? I want to go outside."

Jimmy fumbled with the keys. "I think it's this one," he said and the family went through the door at the far end of the room that led into the kitchen.

At this moment, Lizzie stopped. "Oh, a modern kitchen with a larder and an electric cooker." She could not contain her excitement and she threw her arms around Jimmy. "Let's go into the garden."

Jimmy opened the frosted glass door that had an iron framework that continued along the kitchen window. They all went outside to the muddy mess with large concrete posts with wire stretched between them, separating the garden boundaries.

"It's the Pondarosa," cried Lizzie, and it did look just like the cowboy ranch on Bonanza, a television show she loved.

Lizzie and Jimmy gazed into what seemed like a wilderness, watching their children run around in circles chasing each other, until Jimmy said, "Let's look upstairs."

They turned and went back into the kitchen to investigate the door at the other end of the room. It led to the lobby, a coalhouse, and finally the back door, which led them back to the front street. As Lizzie passed through, she said, "Look Jimmy," pointing to the alcove next to the door. "It's a bin cupboard!"

They all laughed and ran back into the house at the front door to climb up the stairs to check out the three bedrooms, bathroom and separate toilet. Everyone was fascinated with the inside toilet... no more outside visits to the cold lavatory at the bottom of the yard or using potties from under the bed if you needed to go through the night. Sheer luxury, thought Lizzie as she watched her children argue over who was going to have which bedroom. She soon settled that dispute by putting claim to the one with a built-in wardrobe as her own.

She then proceeded to tell Daniel that he would have the small bedroom, as he was the youngest. Daniel happily ran into it and looked out of the window into the garden below.

"I'd like to live here, Jimmy. Would you?"

Jimmy nodded in agreement. "We'll make plans for the move and let the council know so that we can have a date."

Over the weeks that followed the family made plans for the move. Jimmy was now settled into his job as a coach driver with trips up and down the country. He was able to make use of any spare seats by taking along the family, and a favourite of these was a Saturday trip to Blackpool. On one occasion the whole back seat was spare and Jimmy suggested that Mary and Daniel could bring along two friends each. They decided to bring the three Jackson brothers who they played with and Lawrence Baker. Mary was not worried that there was no girlfriend for her as she enjoyed the company of these boys and always joined in their games.

When the day came around, they took turns on the donkeys at Blackpool Beach and the day was taken up at the fun house in the amusement arcade. Best of all was the Tower Ballroom at night where they danced the night away with the young and old to the dance band that played until after midnight. No one was ready to return to the bus to get home late into the evening, least of all Jimmy who had to keep awake for the long drive back to South Shields.

A new life started in Whiteleas with the many party nights that took place, drinking Jimmy's home brew with his loud driver mates from Hall Brother's coaches. By far the most boisterous of these was Jackie Charlton, a young vibrant twenty eight year old who had moved to Whiteleas with his young family of two daughters. His wife was a fiery redhead called Martha, with a temper that made up for her tiny frame. She kept Jackie in line; his 6ft 2ins nineteen stone frame dwarfed her in stature only. They proved to be a good match for Lizzie and Jimmy and it was not long before they made a foursome, spending many weekend nights out in the bars in South Shields.

Jimmy's paraffin business folded as there was little demand for this type of fuel and sadly he reluctantly gave in and concentrated on one job.

Lizzie was happy with her life. The children were growing up fast with Mary now thirteen years old and Daniel eleven. They had established themselves with the gangs of children who had settled on this new council estate. Lizzie befriended a neighbour who lived a few doors away called Kathleen. She was a few years younger than Lizzie and she had four sons, all under six years old.

Lizzie spent quite a few hours a day chatting with her about their lives, and it soon became apparent that Kathleen was bored with her life.

"Ken hates going out. All he does is work and sleep," she confided in Lizzie.

Lizzie thought for a moment and then said, "Why don't you come along for a drink of home brew when Jimmy has his mates along?" Ending her sentence, she laughed with a wink in her eye.

"I might take you up on that. Give me a knock next time," laughed Kathleen with every intention of adding a little spice to her life.

The following weekend, the opportunity came. Lizzie quickly ran along the doors to invite Kathleen down to hers. She knocked on the door and walked straight inside her hallway, calling, "Yoo hoo, only me," keeping her voice as quiet as possible now that Ken would be home.

Kathleen jumped out of her seat to stop Lizzie coming into her sitting room to give the game away.

"Shush," said Kathleen as she came into the kitchen to stop Lizzie in her tracks.

Lizzie had to laugh seeing her friend covering her mouth with her index finger.

"He's stuck in front of that television again, boring old fart," Kathleen whispered.

Lizzie again laughed. "Want to pop along? The lads have arrived. Should be a good night."

Kathleen nodded and went back into her room to speak to Ken. "The bairns are in bed. I'm just going along the doors with Lizzie for a cuppa." She stared at Ken for some sort of reaction.

Ken was almost horizontal, stretched out on the

armchair, resting his hands over his fat belly. He made only a slight effort to turn his head away from the television set he was glued to. Kathleen watched him nod and she turned tail to join her friend Lizzie.

The two friends linked arms and ran down the street laughing until they reached the back door of Lizzie's house where Jimmy was sorting out the barrel of home brew.

Kathleen smiled at Jimmy. "Hope you don't mind me joining the party."

Jimmy was feeling relaxed as he was now well into his third pint of his very strong brew. "Always happy to have a bonny face join us," he said and as he made this final comment, he glanced Kathleen up and down, letting her know he was admiring her trim figure. Jimmy was careful to keep his eyes turned away from Lizzie while he made this pass.

He had not had an affair for quite some time and did not want to spoil anything before it had got started by sending out the warning signals to Lizzie. Kathleen made no attempt to acknowledge this pass while in view of Lizzie. But before she followed her friend into the kitchen, she made sure that she brushed her body past his and looked into his eyes with a knowing look. Jimmy was hooked. All he had to do now was start planning his web of deceit.

Chapter 20

The atmosphere that night was relaxed and fun. Lizzie loved the company of the bus drivers and was pleased that her friend had joined them.

Jimmy waited to make his move until the end of the evening when he heard Kathleen say to Lizzie she was off home.

Lizzie waved to her friend. "See you tomorrow."

Jimmy got up from his chair, saying, "I'll see you out. I'm just about to top my beer up." He then added, "Anyone else want a top up?" No one took any notice, which meant he could get on with his plan.

He followed Kathleen into the lobby, shutting the door behind him. He grabbed her by the arm, turning her towards him. Kathleen immediately took the lead and reached on her tiptoes so that their lips could meet. Jimmy fondled as much of her body that time would allow before they both parted, knowing that they would be spending plenty of time lusting over each other in the weeks that followed.

As she was leaving, Jimmy took a scribbled note out of his pocket and put it in her hand, clenching her fist together to hide it. She made no effort to read it, as time would not permit. She quickly turned to leave the house of her friend and without looking back, she ran along the street to return to her husband.

She opened her back door as quietly as possible, knowing that he would by now be in bed asleep. All the lights were out so she turned on the little lamp that sat on a corner table next to the armchair. She fumbled with the note that Jimmy had squashed into her hand. Excitedly she looked at the note which read, 'Thursday 2pm 38 John Reid Road'.

The following day, Kathleen returned to her friend's house, as she did not wish her to suspect anything of the previous night's event. As she popped her head around the door, she called out in a light-hearted, friendly manner.

Lizzie responded, shouting from upstairs that she was on her way down. She was in good spirits and began to tell Kathleen that she had taken a few shillings from Jimmy's pocket of change.

Kathleen laughed loudly, adding, "Well, if the daft buggers drink so much, they deserve to lose a few bob."

"Well, it'll buy a couple of loaves of bread," Lizzie continued.

The girls laughed as they sat down to a cup of tea.

On Thursday morning, Jimmy told Lizzie that he was picking up his mother to drop her off at the pictures for the afternoon. Lizzie smiled as she was used to Jimmy doing his bit for his mother since his father had died. The old woman was lonely and seemed lost without his support around the house. Jimmy got very frustrated with his mother, but Lizzie noticed he seemed to encourage these trips to the pictures.

Jimmy had his own key and was very irritated if his mother wasn't ready at the agreed time. But as he pulled up his car and looked across the grass verge, he saw the net curtains close so he knew that she would be ready. He quickly walked across the grass and got his key out to open the front door into the small hallway of the bungalow.

His mother was putting the pin into her hat to secure it on her head. "I'm all ready," she said.

Jimmy smiled and picked up her black handbag from the couch next to her to her gloves. "Come on, mam, it's your favourite Humphrey Bogart film."

His mother smiled, thinking what a good son he was to put himself out like this.

When Jimmy returned to the house, Kathleen was waiting uncomfortably at the door. He dashed across the grass verge and said, "Sorry, I had to take me mam to the pictures."

Kathleen smiled. "So it's ya mother's house, is it?"

Jimmy made no comment and took her by the hand, leading her inside and to the bedroom.

They were both experienced lovers and wasted no time or embarrassment in the following hour of lust. After a cigarette, Jimmy opened the bedroom windows wide to get rid of the smells and Kathleen carefully made the bed so that there were no tell tale signs of their activities.

"Will you need a lift?" asked Jimmy, knowing that it would run the risk of someone seeing them.

"No thanks, Jimmy. Best not," she replied.

"Well, close the door behind you," he said. "I have to get away now because I don't want my mother to have to stand around on her own waiting."

Again they smiled and Jimmy left her, knowing she could keep quiet. She had obviously done this before, he thought to himself.

As the weeks went on, the affair continued with Jimmy and Kathleen exchanging confidences, however they both knew it would lead nowhere.

This was only an affair...

As summer approached, the women in Turner Avenue began to sit out on their front steps enjoying the sunshine and a bit of gossip with the folk passing by to go to the shops. Lizzie did not like the sun and she was self conscious of her large figure and ample breasts, which she kept covered. Kathleen, on the other hand, loved the sun and enjoyed the opportunity to wear the skimpy clothes of summer and the short skirts that the sixties brought into fashion. She boosted her tan with a make-up of her own mixture of olive oil and vinegar to boost her colour but which made her smell of fish and chips.

One bright day, Jimmy finished work early and was feeling in a particularly bad mood from a secret which Kathleen had opened his ear to about Lizzie. He was keen to get home and confront her, but knew this would be difficult because of his source.

As he entered the kitchen, Lizzie was preparing the dinner. She turned towards him and knew something was wrong.

"Dinner in about half an hour, Jimmy," she said, making the statement as if to please him.

"I want a word with you," he snapped. "I checked my change in the pocket of my black trousers from Saturday night and I'm short."

Lizzie froze, trying hard to think of what to say. More importantly, she had been doing this for years without Jimmy knowing. She knew something was up. She stared him straight in the eye and said, "I'm not going to deny I take a couple of shillings for bread. You've never noticed before so you know the amount has been small." She continued to stare at him and as she gathered her thoughts, it came to her that the only person she had told was Kathleen.

"You bastard, you're at it again, aren't you, and with Kathleen," she screamed. "I don't know how you have the time but I'm going along there to sort her out."

Jimmy was flabbergasted and was unable to defend himself. He had gone to the house on the attack and she had shot him down. What made it worse was that she was right.

"Don't be ridiculous," he bellowed. "You'll show us all up. She's your mate. What do you think I am?"

Lizzie was in full swing. "I know you, Jimmy Smith."

Her voice was deep and controlled. "You're a whoremaster and I've lived with you too long not to know what you're up to."

Jimmy was speechless.

She knew by his reaction she was right and pushed past him to go to Kathleen's house along the doors. She was fuming by the time she got there. Lizzie paused for a moment, wondering whether to enter as she could hear voices in the kitchen, so for the first time since befriending Kathleen she knocked on the front door.

Within minutes, Ken opened it. "Lizzie, come in," he said. "Is the back door locked?"

Lizzie was never a woman to mince her words or think before she spoke, and rather than enter the house she stood at the doorstep. "Did you know your wife is having an affair with my husband?"

Ken took a step back, knowing that she could be right as he had read the signs too. "You better come in, Lizzie. I don't want the neighbours to hear that sort of talk."

Lizzie, surprised by his reaction, was quick to realise this was not the first time he'd had to deal with this type accusation. She went into the house and found that Kathleen had been listening from behind the door. She'd heard every word and quickly put in, pleading, "How could you think I would do that to you?"

Lizzie snarled back at her, "I trusted you. I told you things I would never even tell my sisters. It could only have been you who told Jimmy about the money."

Gasping for breath, she hissed, "I know you're having it off with him."

Ken was clearly livid by now and said, "Right, I'm having no more of this. Is Jimmy in now, Lizzie."

Lizzie took a deep breath and nodded.

Ken pushed past her to march down the street but Lizzie was right behind him saying, "I know I'm right. I'm never wrong where that whoremaster's concerned."

Ken ignored her comments and knocked on her back door. Jimmy was behind it, getting a shovel full of coal for the fire. He opened the door, looked at Ken and put the shovel back into the coalhouse.

"What's up?" asked Jimmy.

Ken said, "Can I come in, Jimmy? I have something to ask you."

Jimmy nodded and walked into the kitchen, followed by Ken and Lizzie.

"Are you having an affair with my wife?" Ken stared at Jimmy with a pleading look that Jimmy hated in a man.

Jimmy stood his ground. "You don't want to take any notice of Lizzie. She's twisted. She's jealous of everybody and I can't move without her thinking I'm with someone else."

Ken took another deep breath. "I asked you a question."

Jimmy relaxed his shoulders and shook his head as if to say, how could you think that.

But Ken kept on. "Tell me the truth, Jimmy. I need to know."

Jimmy meekly answered, "No."

Lizzie screamed, "You bloody liar, Jimmy Smith," and she elbowed her way past him, knocking into the chair as she stormed upstairs to cool down.

Ken left the scene, knowing that he could not have faced the answer if it had been any different. He returned home without making any comment to Kathleen. He knew if it was an affair, it would come to an end now.

Jimmy went back in the lobby for the coal and banked up the fire. Lizzie stayed in bed. There was no point in saying any more. She knew from past experience that Jimmy liked the chase and that they would be back to normal on Saturday night. They had made plans to meet Jackie and Martha for a drink in the town and the foursome always had a good night together. Her friendship with Kathleen was now over. Lizzie told herself she would get over it one more time. After all, where could she go? She was trapped.

When Saturday came around, the group piled into Jimmy's little red Mini. The suspension on the car could hardly take the weight of their bodies and each time they rode over a bump in the road, they almost hit their heads on the roof. This caused great laughter and a good start to the night of hard drinking.

Lizzie decided early on that she would drink Cherry Bs and Martha went on brandy and Babycham as they could keep up with the pace of rounds the men were setting. At the end of the night, the four friends piled into the Mini with great difficulty as the drink had taken effect on them long before closing time.

"Come back for some home brew," shouted Jimmy as he struggled to get the key into the ignition. He pulled out the choke and revved up the engine to get it started and they all began to sing at the top of their voices while Jimmy swerved about the road on the drive home.

Home brew was always a favourite to end off the night and when it finally came to an end, Jimmy made love to Lizzie to reassure them both that life was back to normal.

The following month, Lizzie began to worry that she had missed a period.

"Maybe you're in the change," said her sister Gracie reassuringly but Lizzie had her doubts.

"Must have been those Cherry Bs and Babychams," answered Lizzie to make a joke of it. But secretly she was terrified. She knew her life with Jimmy would deteriorate if she had another child but the thought of abortion repulsed her.

"Everything happens for a reason," she added, trying to reassure herself.

Throughout the pregnancy, Lizzie suffered panic attacks and often, when she was taking their newly-acquired dog out for a walk, she would shake from underneath her breasts to the pit of her stomach. She would feel the palms of her hands become sweaty and she felt light-headed. If she could run away, this would be one of those times.

Mary was almost fifteen and was due to leave school, but the art teacher had suggested to her and another girl in the class that they should both consider art school. Mary was so excited and could hardly wait to get home and tell her mother the good news.

Lizzie listened as her daughter began to tell her about a future in art school and could only think about her own dilemma and the pregnancy she had to deal with.

"Mary, you can't go to art school. You know how you like your clothes and make-up; you will have to get a job. I'm pregnant. I can't afford to keep you while you go on to further education! It's impossible. You'll have to work."

Mary said nothing. She didn't feel she was being let down as she knew what her mother was saying was right. All the girls she knew were going to leave school to work. She knew no one who went to university or continued their education after they were fifteen. She smiled at her mother in agreement and the subject was never discussed again.

Within two months Mary had her first interview at a solicitor's office and was soon a working girl, paying board money and making new friends.

Lizzie gave birth to a healthy nine and half pound baby girl, which they called Deborah, after the actress Deborah Kerr. Jimmy came to the hospital and it was clear to him that his nose would be pushed out again. Although Jimmy loved his family, he was not a supportive father who became involved in the rounds of feeding and nappy changing and he certainly never once got up to give Lizzie a break from a night feed.

Lizzie soon began to feel isolated and knew that her marriage would be on a downward slide as the months went on. She found solace in her neighbours and began to accept that her and Jimmy were leading separate lives. Her weight ballooned which she simply blamed on middle age and having a baby late in life. She took all Jimmy's remarks about it on the chin and made no effort to change. The party nights with the bus drivers continued and soon she was known as Laughing Lizzie with the young face and the old figure. No one meant any harm by this and Lizzie was the last one to worry, she was too busy getting on with life.

Then one day as Lizzie was sitting down with a cup of tea reading the Gazette from the previous evening, she froze as she read an advert, not believing what she was seeing... someone was asking the whereabouts of Jimmy Smith.

Chapter 21

Lizzie felt a throbbing in her chest and pins and needles in her fingers. Surely it can't be him, she thought to herself, it's a common name, surely not.

She read it again. The contact was made from a person in Stoke-on-Trent. She kept open the page to show Jimmy when he came home, waiting for her moment when the house was quiet and Jimmy had finished his meal.

"What do you think of this?" she asked and placed the folded Gazette in front of his face.

Jimmy leaned back in the chair so that he could focus on the writing. He was clearly stunned and made no attempt to explain. Instead, he said, "I think I had better get in touch with the person and find out what it's about."

"You mean you know someone from Stoke-on-Trent?" asked Lizzie, more puzzled than ever.

"You better sit down, Lizzie. There's something I never told you about my past."

Lizzie felt the sides of her neck throb and she knew she was turning red.

Jimmy waited until she settled down opposite him. Then he came straight to the point. "You know I've been married before Lizzie."

Lizzie's face screwed up. "Married before... yes, I know

that," but before she could say another word he put in, "Lizzie, I know I was wrong not to tell you but it was in the war, I was a young soldier and she got pregnant."

"Pregnant?" Lizzie almost screamed and then calmed down in case she woke her young daughter.

Jimmy continued, "I'm sorry, Lizzie. I know I should have told you. She met an American soldier and she took our daughter with her. I came back up north and never made contact again, only to sign divorce papers."

Lizzie leaned back in the chair, unable to speak. She knew this sort of thing had gone on in the war; she had spoken often enough to her older sisters who had many similar stories to tell about their friends.

"What are you going to do, Jimmy?" she said, staring at him and waiting for his comment.

"Well, you're a part of this now... what do you think I should do?" Jimmy knew if he put the ball in her court, she would throw it right back to him.

"It's nothing to do with me," she stated. "You do what you want, but if you think you're going down there, I'm coming with you."

Jimmy nodded. "Well, I'll write a letter and we'll see what happens."

Jimmy posted the letter the following day and waited. Lizzie was waiting for the post every day for the reply, but it was over two weeks before they heard anything.

When the letter arrived, it was in his first wife's

handwriting, which Jimmy confirmed as he looked over the front of the envelope.

"Well, open it, Jimmy," Lizzie said impatiently.

Jimmy's thick fingers struggled to open the envelope, which was sealed down with sellotape. Lizzie waited patiently while he read the paragraphs until he told Lizzie the contents.

"She's married again, happily from what she says. It's our daughter who has asked her to contact me as she is married and has three sons who she would like to meet their real grandfather." Jimmy paused for breath. "She's asked me to go down to Stoke to meet her."

Before Jimmy could carry on Lizzie put in, "Well, you know what I said. If you go, I go too."

Jimmy nodded in agreement. He was curious. They discussed whether they should tell the children and decided it would be best to be truthful.

That evening at the dinner table, Jimmy explained about the advert in the Gazette asking to trace him and that they would be going to Stoke to meet his previous family. Daniel made no comment, which was usual for him in his quiet unconcerned manner; all he hoped was that it would not affect him. Mary, on the other hand, was quite excited at the idea of having an older sister and said she would like to write to her. Jimmy and Lizzie felt happy in their decision to go to Stoke, which was agreed would happen the following weekend he had free.

The travel down was one of apprehension and the closer they got to their destination, the more Lizzie's nerves played up, making her visit the toilet at every available opportunity. Jimmy was surprised that Stoke had not changed very much as he easily found his way to the agreed meeting place, a corner cafe he used to frequent as a young soldier.

He spotted Sonia sitting quietly in the corner with a much older gentleman. As he made his way down the aisle, Lizzie kept close by his side. She noticed the lady get up out of her seat and stare attentively at Jimmy.

That must be her, she thought to herself.

Jimmy called out her name and she responded by extending out her hand to shake his. Jimmy immediately turned around to introduce Lizzie.

The two women smiled at each other and shook hands, which only left the final introduction of the elderly gentleman who was left sitting on his own in the corner.

"Jimmy, this is my husband, Brian," Sonia said.

Brian rose from his seat and extended his warm handshake. "Please sit down." He pointed to the chairs opposite inviting them to sit down. "What can I get you to drink? You must be exhausted from the early morning start you will have had to make. Would you like a meal? Please, sit, it will be my pleasure." He handed them the café menu.

Lizzie smiled at this warm-hearted elderly gentleman who did not have an American accent.

They glanced over the menu and decided on fish and

chips, with bread and butter, which was a special on the menu that day. Lizzie felt warmed by his generosity but was not at all sure about Sonia's motives. However, Sonia dispelled her thoughts by immediately telling Jimmy about how much his daughter had been asking both her and Brian about her real father. "I'm so sorry to bring you both on this journey but she has gone on about this since she had a third child. Which, Jimmy, I have to tell you before you decide to meet them all…" She paused. "… the baby, Stephen she has called him, is brain damaged."

Jimmy stopped putting the fish in his mouth and pondered for a moment. "In what way is his brain damaged?" he asked, by now almost totally put off his dinner.

"Well, he's deaf and blind. He was premature and they said at the hospital this was the most likely cause. Anne has suffered from depression ever since."

The conversation ended. Lizzie was reluctant to speak and was having a hard time trying to follow the situation they found themselves in.

Sonia again took the lead. "Well, let's finish our dinners and you can let me know how you feel about the meeting when it's had time to sink in."

The group bent their heads down to look into the meal in front of them and tried to eat with some sort of enthusiasm. Brian tried to lighten up the conversation by asking them about their journey, and if Jimmy had time to notice any of the changes that had taken place in Stoke since he left.

Jimmy shook his head. "Not really, we haven't had much time to look around."

Brian nodded and as he did, he smiled across at Lizzie, hoping she would add to the conversation, but she could not think of anything to say.

When the last drop of tea had been drunk from the large pot, Sonia looked around and indicated it was time to leave by turning in her chair to pick up her coat.

Brian stood and took it from her to hold it open so that she could slip her right arm into the sleeve opening. Jimmy and Lizzie pushed the wooden chairs out of the way so that they could follow the couple they had come so far to meet.

As they crossed the road, Jimmy took hold of Lizzie's hand and squeezed it tight, trying to reassure her and let her know that he was pleased she was with him. He watched Brian open the door of his Rover 90. A working man's Rolls Royce, Jimmy thought to himself with slight envy. They all got into the Rover and sank into the comfortable leather seats until Brian turned over the engine and carefully pulled out of the parking place to begin their journey.

It took about fifteen minutes to reach Anne's house. Lizzie took notice of the estate with modern suburban semi's with neatly kept lush green lawns which looked like thick green blankets dividing the open plan properties. As they approached the house, Lizzie felt herself sighing, and Jimmy again took hold of her hand to reassure her.

They all got out of the Rover together and followed Sonia up the path towards the front door which was framed by two large plant pots containing geraniums, pansies and a miniature conifer. Sonia rang the doorbell and waited.

Lizzie wondered why she could not knock and enter, as she would have done to a member of her own family, especially a daughter. After some minutes, the door was opened by a small-framed young lady with hair that was short and cropped, framing a small pretty face. A baby was sitting on her hip, smiling at the group. The young woman made no attempt to hug anyone and it looked as though the child was used as a barrier to keep a distance between them. Sonia moved forward and kissed her daughter on the cheek, Brian followed and did the same. Anne then moved to the side to allow Jimmy and Lizzie to come inside.

Jimmy felt very uncomfortable and unsure whether to carry on the ritual with a kiss on the cheek. He stood for a moment, but Anne only indicated to go inside.

Lizzie followed uncomfortably.

Sonia again took the lead. "I'll pop the kettle on," she said, "and then we can all get to know each other."

Everyone looked around and took a seat without speaking.

Brian said, "Well, make yourselves comfortable," looking to Anne in the hope that she would join in the conversation.

She said nothing and began to turn the baby around

on her lap to face her. She continued to make faces at the baby, without acknowledging Brian.

Lizzie decided to get out of her seat and made her way across the room towards the child. "What do you call him?" she asked.

"Stephen," was Anne's formal reply.

Lizzie took his tiny hand and tried to make contact with his face, leaning over to try to speak to him.

"He's deaf," was Anne's cold comment as she turned her eyes towards Jimmy, making him feel very uncomfortable.

"Can he see?" asked Lizzie.

"Yes, he can see shapes. That's why I turned him around to see my face."

"Can I hold him?" asked Lizzie.

Anne looked towards her, surprised by the warmth. She reluctantly lifted up the child for Lizzie to hold. Lizzie immediately took the child and freely gurgled with him in her arms while the group looked on without saying a word.

Holding the child in her arms gave Lizzie a sense of security, so she continued with her gurgled communication. After a few moments, the scene was interrupted by Sonia carrying a large tray containing tea, biscuits and cake.

As she placed the tray on the table, she turned towards her daughter and looked in Jimmy's direction. "Well, Jimmy, this is your daughter, Anne. I expect it's a bit of a shock, not seeing her since she was two."

Jimmy smiled and got up from his seat. He leaned across to Anne and took her hand. "I'm sorry it's taken so long for us to meet. I'm afraid the war has a lot to answer for." He hoped this final comment would release him from the guilt he was feeling and waited for Anne to make a kind gesture in agreement.

She only smiled and shook his hand. "We have a lot to catch up on. Perhaps we can start writing to each other?"

"Oh yes," said Jimmy, absolutely relieved. "I have another daughter who would love to hear from you. Would you like to write to her as well?"

Anne smiled. "Yes, my mother told me about your new family."

"She's called Mary," Jimmy added.

"My mother said you have a younger daughter as well, but I suppose she's too young to write just yet!"

Everyone laughed and it appeared that the ice was broken.

The afternoon went well considering the enormity of the meeting. Sonia's final words to Jimmy, as the company parted for their journeys home was, "Well, I'll write to you, Jimmy, and keep you updated."

Jimmy nodded and as he did, he looked across at Lizzie, wondering how that final comment would be taken. Lizzie ignored the remark and presumed this was how it was if you had a previous family. They lived far enough away not to cause any problems, she thought to herself and ignored her warning bells.

When they returned home, Mary and Daniel were waiting to hear the news about their stepsister, who had three children. Jimmy informed Mary that she would like to write to her and said that she may like to send some photos.

Mary smiled; she loved writing letters and already had three pen pals across the world. Daniel quietly turned away, glad that his father had not included him in the writing exercise.

Over the next few months, the letters and photographs continued until Jimmy asked Mary to stop. But when he gave no explanation, Mary asked her mother what the problem was.

"I don't know, pet," said Lizzie, secretly relieved that any contact with Jimmy's past family was now over. "Probably for the best. You have plenty of other friends to write to."

Mary nodded in agreement, a bit sad at the thought of losing touch with the sister she'd just found, but not wanting to upset her mam and dad.

Jimmy, however, as much as he'd suggested his daughter stop writing, had not himself stopped keeping up with his own letters and was now communicating with Sonia using his mother's address at John Reid Road. His mother made no effort to ask why the letters were coming to her house. None of my business, she told herself.

Jimmy reassured himself there would never be any way that he could be found out, knowing Lizzie had never renewed the friendship with his mother. It was a perfect arrangement.

As the months went by, Jimmy began to look at his wife with contempt as he imagined what life could be like again with Sonia. He could find nothing attractive in Lizzie; her weight was out of control, and he hated her short lifeless hair. She had no smart clothes and wore the same stretch black trews, alternated with a brown pair every day. She had a couple of worn-out jumpers and she constantly wore a pair of slippers, even wearing them to walk to the local shops. This infuriated him, though many women on the estate did their shopping wearing slippers. It seemed more important to women to wear a headscarf or woolly hat on their heads than to wear a pair of shoes on their feet to do their daily shopping.

It never once occurred to Jimmy that he could buy her some clothes, instead he told her that she should get a job if she could not manage on the housekeeping money he gave her.

Gradually Lizzie realised that she would have to try and get some money for herself and when the opportunity came to look after a neighbour's child while she went to work, Lizzie jumped at the chance.

She was home looking after her young daughter, and her grown up family spent most of their time either at work or out with their own friends. Perhaps this was just what she needed, she thought to herself. She spent the next three years looking after the neighbour's child until he and her own daughter were settled into school life.

Before long, Lizzie missed the little extra she'd been

making and decided she must get herself a real job. Her family all got themselves up for work and even her youngest daughter was so independent she was able to get herself off to school with very little assistance from Lizzie. She began to ask in the local shops for a part time job and as she was buying some mince one day, she overheard a lady talking of a cook's job in the assessment home for children that had recently opened next to the shops.

Lizzie boldly turned and joined in the conversation, "When did you hear about it?" she interrupted.

The ladies turned towards her and gladly gave all the information Lizzie needed. She smiled, thanking them, and left the shop to make enquiries. She only had to walk a hundred yards to reach the front door of the home where she bravely rang the bell and waited.

The door was opened slowly and a lady wearing a green overall peeped around it while still holding the side of the door with her right hand as if to protect herself. She looked Lizzie up and down, wondering if she was a parent making enquiries.

"I've come about the cook's job," Lizzie blurted out before the lady had a chance to speak.

"Oh," was the reply as the lady smiled, opening the door wide and inviting Lizzie to enter by the open gesture of her arm. "Just along the corridor," she said. "Mrs Armstrong's office is at the end. The door's always open… she'll be at her desk."

Lizzie walked along and found Mrs Armstrong looking

up from her bespectacled face, wondering who she would be interviewing now.

"Come in," she welcomed. "Sit down and tell me what your experience is."

Lizzie sat down, feeling very uncomfortable and wondering what she could say.

Mrs Armstrong watched Lizzie carefully and waited for her response.

"Well, I've mainly worked in shops but for the past three years or so I've been looking after a neighbour's child, along with my own. I do my own cooking and I'm sure I could cook for a few more bairns."

Mrs Armstrong did not speak for a moment as she took an immediate liking to this burly woman. She looked ideal for the job and her jovial exterior would be ideal for the type of children that came into the home.

Finally, she answered Lizzie. "Well, I've interviewed a few for the job, but between you and me, they were a bit above themselves. Of course, I haven't said that. I think you'll fit in fine here, Lizzie. When can you start?"

Lizzie's eyebrow raised, making creases appear in her forehead and when she finally opened her mouth, she found herself taking a breath that felt like a sigh of relief.

"Monday, if you like. What time?" she asked.

Mrs Armstrong's tone changed to a business-like manner. "I would need you here prompt 6.45am to prepare breakfast for twelve children. The tables are set for them to sit down at 7.30am. Sometimes we only have two or three children for assessment but at the moment we're full. You would then prepare the dinner for twelve and tea before you left." She paused. "Tea is mainly sandwiches and crisps and you could make a cake… they all like cakes for tea. You would finish and after that your time is yours to manage. As long as the meals are done, your day is over." She waited and as there was no response from Lizzie, she said, "See you Monday."

Lizzie rose from the chair, smiling apprehensively as she tried to imagine herself working there.

At dinner that night, she told the family and received little response, only her daughter Mary saying, "That's great, mam. I can see the bairn off to school in the mornings before I get my bus to work."

Then just as if nothing had been said, everyone carried on with dinner.

Chapter 22

Life was becoming strained but Lizzie was too busy working to notice how far apart Jimmy was moving from her. She thought his affairs had ended and imagined he was past it.

But they barely spoke unless it was to argue and this was always over meals that were not ready for him or not what he expected to eat when he came in from work, whatever time it was after a long day's shift.

Mary hated it, hated the rows and hated how her dad was treating her mam. One night, when she was returning home from the Hedworth Hall where she had been out with her friends dancing, it all came to a head. The girls always walked home together, chattering away the time about the important things in their lives, which was mainly clothes and boyfriends and when they could leave home and get a flat of their own.

Mary said goodnight to her friends at the corner of her street and proceeded to take the short walk home. As she got closer to her house, she could hear her parents shouting at the top of their voices. The back door must be open, she thought as she shuddered, looking around the neighbouring houses to see if anyone was looking out of their windows.

Suddenly, she saw her father run out of the house.

He stopped dead on the lawn, turned his head back to the house and shouted, "That's the last fry up you'll do for me."

Mary stopped in her tracks as she witnessed the pan being hurled with as much force as he could muster to pelt it up the street. She waited, unable to move a step forward, wondering if her mother would be dragged out next.

There was a silence, followed by the slamming of the back door. Mary slowly put one foot in front of the other as she desperately hoped that none of the neighbours were watching out of their windows. She tried not to look as the net curtains moved back and forth from the folk that knew everyone's business on this new council estate.

She entered the house that was deathly silent, passed her mother boiling potatoes and looked at her father in disgust as he continued to read his paper as if nothing had happened.

Mary would leave for London with her friend just after her eighteenth birthday.

Lizzie always believed in her daughter and held her head high as she told friends and neighbours how well Mary was doing in London... until one day when she was stopped in the street by the woman whose daughter had gone to London with Mary.

"Well," she muttered as she approached Lizzie, "our Judith has written to us to tell us that Mary is living with her boyfriend."

Lizzie was speechless. "What do you mean? I thought she lived with your Judith," she uttered indignantly.

"Well, it seems they fell out because of him being there all the time and our Judith left them to it."

Lizzie ignored the comment and continued to make her way into the house as if the statement was made about someone else. But that night she was forced to speak to Jimmy and ask what they could do.

"Well, you better write to her and find out what's going on," was his only reply.

Lizzie went straight to the bureau. "I'm taking some of your writing paper to write today," and with that comment she went into the kitchen to put pen to paper.

But when she sat down, it was very hard to think of the right words and all she wrote was: 'We know you are living with Johnny Carter. He will never marry you now. Your dad and me are disgusted. We have always put you on a pedestal. We expected better of you.'

Lizzie signed the letter, sealed the envelope and trooped off to the post office in her slippers for a stamp to post the letter.

When Mary received the letter the following day, she was heartbroken. Her boyfriend rang his parents from the phone box and said they would be getting married next week if they could get a license.

"What about witnesses?" his mother cried.

"We'll get a couple off the street," he said. "We're only having a wedding for us, not everybody else."

His mother's pleas continued until he finally told her his money had run out and that he would ring them back with a date for the registry office.

Four days later, Lizzie received a letter from her daughter saying simply: 'Johnny and I will be getting married in Fulham Registry Office next Saturday. If you want to come, you're welcome.'

Lizzie did not make any comment as she handed over the brief letter that was addressed to them both.

Jimmy read it and, thinking the whole thing would cost him too much money, stated firmly to Lizzie, "I'm not going."

Lizzie answered, "Well, I'll go myself with the bairn."

No more was spoken of the day she spent in London watching her daughter marry a man she knew was not right for her. She'll have to make her own mistakes just like I have, Lizzie thought to herself, only this time I hope she's wiser than me.

Lizzie and Jimmy continued living separate lives, not realising how bad things were getting.

Then one day, Lizzie got home from work early to find a note pushed in her door asking for her to contact the hospital. She had no idea who it was from but promptly left the house to go and ask her neighbour Irene if she could use her telephone. Irene loved a bit of intrigue and scandal was even better for her appetite. However, on this occasion she felt worried for her friend as she dialled the number and asked to be put through the extension number written on the note.

Lizzie was asked for identification and to confirm her address and was then asked if she could come down to the hospital immediately as her husband had been admitted.

Irene watched her friend's face drain of colour and waited to be told the outcome as Lizzie put down the telephone.

"Jimmy's in hospital and I've been asked to go straight down," she said.

"What's happened to him?" Irene asked.

"I don't know, they didn't say and I didn't ask," Lizzie continued. "I better get the bus down there."

"Would you like a cuppa before you go? You look like it would do you good… the shock and all," she added.

But Lizzie was opening the front door to leave. "No, I'd better go. I've left the phone money on your little table."

She did not look back or hear her friend say it didn't matter, she just felt herself trying to run along the pavements back home.

When she reached the house, she almost fell into the hallway, picking up her coat from one of the hooks on the wall. She picked up her purse from the table and shuffled around in the drawer of the bureau for a pen and paper to leave a note that she would be back later. She then left the house, leaving the back door on the latch so that it was open for the family coming in at teatime.

Lizzie was out of breath by the time she reached the General Hospital. She gave her brief note to the receptionist who confirmed that Jimmy Smith was in the Intensive Care Ward after suffering a heart attack.

She felt apprehensive as she approached the ward sister who took her along the quiet ward, pointing to where Jimmy was sleeping.

"He's alright," she said. "He got here in the nick of time and we kept him in. He's had a heart attack and is recovering. Don't stay too long as we want him to rest. You can come back tomorrow. He'll be awake then."

And with that, she walked quietly away, leaving Lizzie standing at the bottom of the bed, watching the man she wondered if she still loved. She sniffed, taking in the smell of the ward, and looked at the chair next to his bed, wondering if she should sit down. Turning her head from side to side, there were no other visitors in the ward and all the patients were asleep.

"They don't look long for this world," she muttered to herself and began to wonder if Jimmy was too. He was only fifty-four and Lizzie began to feel guilty as she imagined what it would be like to be a widow.

She moved slowly towards the chair, but did not turn it to face his bed. Instead, she sat facing the bed opposite but out of the corner of her eye, she looked at his hand just peeping through the sleeve of the pyjamas he had on. She took another breath as if gathering up the courage to reach across and hold it. This was the first time she had felt the warmth of his skin in five years.

She felt a lump rising in her throat and an uncontrollable tear trickled down her cheek, which she left to fall from the end of her chin. She sat quietly and then turned towards him. "Looks like you'll be needing me for a while, Jimmy Smith." And with that remark, she got up to leave.

When Lizzie returned home, Daniel had cooked some leftovers from yesterday's Sunday dinner and was washing up.

"The bairn's outside playing, mam. Is everything alright? I just dished up what I could find to eat." Daniel turned towards her and waited for her reply.

Lizzie did not speak at first as she pulled off her coat and walked back into the lobby to hang it up. Just as she was about to put the collar of her coat over the hanger, she blurted out, "Your dad's had a heart attack," and with that she entered the kitchen again.

Daniel watched her face, waiting to be told if it was serious.

She continued, "Well, he seems alright. Was sleeping when I got there. Someone pushed a note in the door, saying I had to contact the hospital."

Daniel answered. "You will have to tell Mary. You can ring the house where her bedsit is and get them to pass a message on." Daniel again watched her as he tried to make the right suggestions to help.

"Yes, I'll do that later," she said. "I'll ask Irene if I can use her phone again."

Daniel told his mam to sit down and he poured her a cup of tea from the pot he'd made. "I'll go down the hospital with you tomorrow after work."

Lizzie nodded to Daniel as she sniffed over her cup of tea.

When Lizzie finally got in touch with her daughter, Mary told her that she would be coming home immediately with her husband at the weekend when they finished work. Lizzie tried to get the house ready by moving the beds around but then decided she would let Mary and Johnny sleep in the back room where Jimmy slept. They had long since slept in different rooms and Lizzie was told from the hospital that he would be in there for at least another week even though he was making excellent progress.

That weekend the whole family sat around Jimmy's bed, smiling at one another as if nothing had ever happened to cause any resentment between them.

Jimmy smiled at his daughter and then said, "You know, Mary, I won't forget your mam for all she has done for me. I know we've had our ups and downs but this time we'll make a fresh start. I nearly died last week and if I hadn't come to the accident and emergency with the gripping pains in my chest, I might not be here to tell the tale. I'll never forget how much sweat came out of my body; my shirt was soaking when they tried to get it off me. Yes, I'm a lucky man."

Lizzie smiled, bathing in the compliment she had just received. Maybe her marriage to Gentleman Jim would work out after all.

When they got home that night, Mary told Johnny that she wanted to come back to South Shields. Even though they were saving all her wages and living on his, she could never save enough to meet the rising house prices in London. Johnny agreed. He had plenty of mates to pick back up with and could live anywhere. Secretly Mary hoped she could make a better life in north. She had nothing in the south and very rarely saw her husband until he came home to eat after he'd had his fill of beer when he came off the building site with his Irish friends who were like-minded people.

To that end, she asked Lizzie if she could get the newspapers so they could look at properties the following weekend.

"I'll tell them at work what I'm doing and that I need my holidays," Mary added.

Lizzie was over the moon. Finally, she was getting her family back. Just the way all mothers should have, she thought, and a daughter to visit, that's the way it should be.

When the weekend came, Mary and Johnny drove up north in their little A40 car and were greeted immediately at the door by Lizzie who shuffled down the path in her slippers to help them out with their cases.

"Your dad's on the couch. You go in. I'll help Johnny with your bags."

Mary rushed in to find her dad had all the papers spread out ready on the floor with properties at prices they could afford.

Lizzie was smiling as she came into the sitting room with Johnny.

"Tea's made," she said and pottered on into the kitchen to bring out a tray of sandwiches and a pot of tea.

Soon they were enjoying a bite to eat while they scanned the papers looking for properties.

"These two sound nice... one in Whitley Bay and another in Wallsend," said Mary, hoping to keep Johnny away from his old drinking mates in South Shields.

"Over the water? Why would you want to live over the water?" asked her Johnny.

"Well, the price is right in both of them. Should we just view them and see what we think when we get there?" she asked in reply.

Everyone nodded in agreement so when tea was over, they decided to contact the estate agent immediately as there was little time to spare. Lizzie busied herself in the kitchen to get a dinner ready for teatime while Jimmy continued reading the paper.

"It will be nice to have them settled up here, Jimmy," Lizzie shouted from the kitchen.

Jimmy muttered some reply through the pipe he was now smoking. He'd been told to give up his cigarettes if he wanted to live any longer. The pipe was no substitute and wasn't helping his mood.

Lizzie ignored him. She had her daughter coming home and that was all that mattered.

As time went by, Lizzie helped as much as she could with the move Mary made from London to settle for a terrace property in Whitley Bay, near the sea front, so much so that Lizzie again failed to realise that Jimmy was losing interest in her now that his strength was coming back. Daniel was spending more time with his girlfriend, and Lizzie's life revolved around her little job and her youngest daughter, Deborah.

"Sent for a purpose," she commented to everyone about her.

To add to her pleasure, Mary announced that she was expecting her first child and when the boy was born, Lizzie felt that her life was fulfilled in becoming a grandmother. She could not get enough of this beautiful boy they called John, after his father. Every weekend she waited to meet them off the ferry so she could look after him overnight on Saturday, and then on Sunday she would take her daughter and grandson back on the ferry which was a ritual she would not have wanted to miss for the world.

But however happy she had become as a grandmother, she was now seeing her daughter Mary in a different light and noticed that she was losing a lot of weight and although she knew that she and Johnny were going out together at weekends, Lizzie could see how his drinking was affecting their marriage.

She kept telling her daughter to go out with him at every opportunity and not to make the same mistakes that she did.

But it seemed to have very little influence on her so

Lizzie satisfied her frustration by defending her daughter at every opportunity and attacking Johnny with as much verbal abuse as she could dish out. They became sparring partners when Johnny had been drinking which was much to his delight, as he enjoyed nothing better than a good argument. It was a thorn in Lizzie's otherwise perfect family, and one she wasn't going to give in to.

Chapter 23

One Saturday afternoon, Mary spent the day with her mother and was waiting for Johnny to pick her up so that they could have their usual night out in Whitley Bay, leaving young John to stay overnight with his grandmother.

When Mary saw the black Capri car pull up outside, she began to sort out the overnight things to leave behind. She turned her head, looking out of the window at her husband and realised from his swagger he was well on the way to being drunk. She dreaded these moments, knowing that he would either pick an argument with her, resulting in an excuse to go out by himself, or he would get home and after eating his freshly cooked rump steak, mushrooms, onions and chips, he'd fall fast asleep on the settee, snoring so loud that it would be pointless waking him. She knew from experience that if she tried that, he'd get into a mood that would again cause another argument to give him a reason to storm off to bed, shouting that he'd been working hard all week and should be allowed rest when he wanted it. Mary knew it would be one of those nights that she would be in a no-win situation.

Lizzie noticed her daughter's anxious look as she turned, glancing briefly at her while she sorted out the baby bag.

"There he is. I'll get the door," said Lizzie, not realising how sternly she had spoken. She opened the door, glaring at her son-in-law as he staggered past her.

"Alright there?" he smiled as he tripped over the small step leading into the house.

Lizzie was furious and gave no reply.

"You ready then?" he asked Mary as she began to fumble around, trying to get everything sorted quickly to get him out of the house as soon as possible.

"I'd love a cup of tea, Lizzie?" Johnny turned, looking Lizzie in the eye, encouraging her to bite at his sarcasm.

"Don't worry, mam," Mary put in. "I'm sorted now and we can get home."

Johnny turned aggressively towards his wife. This was just what he wanted and said, "I'll have a cup of tea, if you don't mind."

Mary took a sharp breath in as she tried to smile and nod at him at the same time.

He continued, "What's the matter with your face? Do you want to get me out of here before I cause a scene? Well, we wouldn't want to do that would we, 'Princess Mary'?"

Lizzie could take no more; she had seen him act like this towards her daughter for the last time. She made her move by standing in front of Mary and faced Johnny full on so that they were eyeballing each other.

Johnny laughed, getting ready for his sparring partner.

Lizzie lurched forward and pointed her finger between his eyes. "Look," she started, "you either want my daughter or you don't. I'm sick of the way you speak to her. What do you want? And if you don't want her…" She paused again then snapped, "Get out of my house and leave her here."

Lizzie hoped this would bring him to his senses.

Mary froze, knowing it wouldn't.

Johnny laughed again in a smug manner, happy this was just what he was hoping for. "That suits me fine," he announced. "You can have them both. I'm off."

And with that, he marched out, leaving Mary dumbfounded as she tried to comprehend that she was now being forced into living back with her parents.

Lizzie was not to be beaten and turning, she said to her daughter, "Let the bugger go. He's not worth shedding a tear over."

Mary dropped her head. "Mam, I've got no clothes or anything here."

"That's alright, our Daniel can take you over tomorrow and you can get what you need."

That night Mary slept in Deborah's bed and she with her mother. John was quite happy in his little carrycot and was none the wiser.

The following morning, Daniel came over in his car to take Mary to Whitley Bay for some things. She didn't know what she needed or for how long and she felt thoroughly dominated by the two people who were at loggerheads with each other over her.

When Daniel pulled up in the car, he was about to get

out when Mary said, "Wait here, Daniel. He may be still in bed."

Daniel paused. "Are you sure?" He looked at his sister with caring eyes. "I'll come in with you."

"No, I'll be fine. He'll have slept it off if he's in there." And with that, she got out of the passenger seat to walk the few short steps to the front door.

She put the key into the lock and, turning it, she walked inside the small passageway. The house seemed cold and dark. As she walked up the stairs, she realised that all the curtains were closed in all the rooms. She quietly entered the bedroom she shared with Johnny and realised the heap of blankets she was looking at had a body underneath with only eyes and nose peeping out from them. The snoring continued as she looked around, wondering what to take and hoping at the same time that her brother would stay outside in the car.

Johnny turned over, sensing that someone was in the room. He slowly opened one eye and seeing Mary, he said, "Oh, you're back. Where's John?" His voice was soft and caring and she heard all the qualities that a loving husband should display when he had almost lost his wife.

"He's at my mam's," she said. "I've just come for a few things to take back."

Johnny pulled himself up quickly now. "What do you mean, 'take back'…?" He sounded shocked and upset, wondering what could have upset her so much that she could think of wanting to go back home. He continued, "You know I didn't mean what I said. She just provokes me. I think she does it on purpose because she wants to break us up." His piercing blue eyes began searching into hers for a weakness.

Mary knew there was a ring of truth in what he said and desperately wanted to believe him in the hope she could have the family life she never had. "What do you mean?" she said, giving him another chance.

This was all he needed and proceeded with his charm until she agreed and went back outside to tell her brother that they had sorted things out and to tell mam she would be coming back within the hour to collect the baby.

Lizzie could say nothing; she knew she had made all these mistakes in her life so she could not condemn her daughter.

Within three months, Johnny had decided it would be a good idea if they got away on their own for a holiday abroad. Although Mary was reluctant, she agreed to have a word with her mother. So when Saturday arrived and she made her weekly visit, she tested the water.

"Mam, I've got a bit favour to ask you…"

Lizzie looked at her daughter, wondering what it could be.

"We have a couple of friends who have asked us to go to Ibiza with them, just for a week," Mary said. "I don't want to leave John but he's too young to take and Johnny is adamant he wants us to go; it will be our first trip abroad. I could only go if you looked after John…" she added reluctantly.

Lizzie let loose of the buggy she was pushing John in and turned to grab her daughter's arms. "You get yourself away. Don't miss out on a chance to go abroad. I can look after John and I can take my own holiday and come to your house with Deborah. We can have our holiday in Whitley Bay." She smiled broadly.

Mary looked at Deborah. "Would you like to come and stay in my house for a week and look after John and go to the beach every day? And…" she added, "you could go and spend the pocket money I give you in the Spanish City on the rides. Would you like that, Deborah?"

Deborah smiled and they all laughed, feeling very excited.

When Lizzie returned home, she expected some protest from Jimmy. He would be left on his own now that Daniel had moved in with his own girlfriend at her mother's house. However, Jimmy's only comment was, "Well, I suppose I can look after myself and the break will do everyone good."

Lizzie smiled, looking forward to the following month when she would be in Whitley Bay for one week.

Jimmy, most of all, was looking forward to it. This was his opportunity to renew an old friendship and consider whether he could change his life once and for all. He wrote his usual letter to Sonia and told her about his daughter's trip to Ibiza and invited her to stay with him in Turner Avenue if she could get away.

The plans were set.

Lizzie loved every minute of her time in Whitley Bay; she enjoyed the sea air and the walks along the promenade every day where they stopped on the way back for a bag of chips to share between them as they made their way home. Lizzie even wondered if she could get a council house exchange to Whitley Bay so that she could be near her daughter and grandchild.

When Mary returned, Lizzie had as much to tell her about her pleasurable holiday as Mary did about hers.

But when Lizzie returned home to Whiteleas, she instinctively knew something was different as she walked in through the back door. Was it the clean smell and the tidiness everywhere she turned...? Even her cupboards had been moved around, with the cups, saucers and plates organised in rotation between the shelves.

She looked around, unsettled. Her furniture had been moved as if someone had removed every item to clean and vacuum in all corners of the room. She slowly climbed the stairs where all the familiar dust had disappeared from the paintwork between the stair rods and carpet. Jimmy would never take the time to do this, she thought. And instead of entering her own room, she opened the door of the small back bedroom and turned back the sheets of his bed...

She stood for a moment, looking at the tell-tale signs of sex, and she froze. How could he bring someone back here? The neighbours would have seen it all but there was no way she was going to ask anyone of them to tell her what had gone on. She could see for herself. So instead of unpacking, she turned around and took Deborah back on the ferry to Whitley Bay.

When she arrived, she found Mary unpacking and washing the rest of her clothes. She felt reluctant at first to tell her daughter but Mary said, "Mam, what's the matter? Have you left something? I've cleared the room and there's nothing there…"

"No, I haven't left anything. Can I have a cup of tea?"

Mary made her way into the kitchen at the back of the house and Lizzie followed. Deborah stayed in the lounge, playing with John. No words were spoken as Mary continued getting out the cups and saucers, until she turned and said gently, "I've still got some fruit cake left. Could you eat a piece, mam?"

Lizzie shook her head, still stuck for words.

Mary waited for her mother to tell her what was wrong and when she finally had the tray prepared, Lizzie said, "Your dad's at it again… he's had someone in the house while I was over here."

Mary felt sick. "How could you know that?" she asked.

"Marks all over the bed, sex marks," Lizzie said, staring at her daughter, hoping to see disgust in her eyes. "You know he's been at it all the time. I know you don't believe me, but our Daniel knows what he's up to, I know he does."

"Mam, what are you going to do?" Mary answered, unable to take in what she was hearing.

"I'm leaving him for good. I'll get in touch with our Sadie in Coventry. I haven't seen my sister for many a year, but as she's a widow I know she won't mind me living there."

Mary stared at her mother. "What about our Deborah, mam?"

Lizzie retorted immediately. "I'll leave her with him. That'll put paid to his antics. He won't be able to carry on with a eight year old to take care of."

Mary looked her mother in the eye and said, "Mam, if you go this time, I'll be taking Deborah in. I'll look after her."

Lizzie's blood ran cold… her own daughter not backing her up after all she had done for her. All the support and babysitting she had done and now she would not back up her plans. "Don't bother with the tea," she said. "I'm going back to confront him."

"Mam, let Deborah stay here tonight so you and dad can work things out better on your own. I'll bring her back tomorrow and you can tell me what you're going to do."

Lizzie did not look back; she simply nodded her head, leaving the house without another word.

Her temper was well and truly fired up by the time she got back to Whiteleas. When she arrived back, she almost knocked the back door off its hinges as she flung it open to march into where Jimmy was sitting, eating a fry up.

He raised his head and looked over the top of his glasses. "Oh, you're back, are you?" he said, folding the newspaper over as if to start a conversation with her.

Lizzie almost bent over the top of him before he could raise himself off the chair. She pointed her index finger menacingly at him and growled in a low guttural voice, "Back? You bastard whoremaster. Back? I bet you wished I'd never come back." She took a deep breath. "So you could carry on with your whoring."

Jimmy tried to remain calm, wondering if the neighbours had got to her already, but before he could drum up a lie, she continued, "I've seen those sheets. I know what you've been doing while I was away," and with that, she pushed him off the chair so that he fell between the cupboard and the dog's bowl. The dog immediately came in from the sitting room and began barking at them both but Jimmy heard nothing, his fury overtook him and he got up to start punching into Lizzie.

She felt nothing as she fell into the open door of the larder, where on the floor next to her was a hammer. She picked it up and went to take a swing at him.

Jimmy was quick to grab her arm and in a single moment, he heard the dog barking furiously between them, making him briefly come to his senses. He took the hammer from Lizzie and immediately started hammering into the sink unit while Lizzie stood back and watched him vent his frustration.

When he finally stopped due to the shortage of breath, Lizzie wondered if he would have another heart attack, but he didn't. Instead, he said to her calmly, "I'll be going to the council tomorrow to get out of here. If I don't, one of us will end up in the grave."

Lizzie was frozen to the spot where he had taken the hammer from her. As Jimmy walked out, the dog began to jump up at her and with an automatic response that belied the turmoil she had inside, she said, "Come on, I'll take you for a walk."

She took his lead from the kitchen drawer and the dog jumped and barked in appreciation as they left the house through the back door.

Jimmy watched her go then went into the sitting room to write a letter to Sonia to let her know what had happened and that they could be together at last, ending with a final sentence that he would be going to the council the following day to register for a council flat.

Mary hardly slept that night as she wondered what was happening with her mother and father. She wished they had a telephone so that she could at least hear their voices. Early the following morning after Johnny had left for work, she got the children ready for the ferry trip across to South Shields. She was not prepared for what lay ahead.

When she arrived at the house, her father was busy setting the fire away.

"Hello, pet," he said. "I'm just heating up some water for a bath."

"Is mam around?" asked Mary, wondering if they had managed to salvage anything from the events.

"No, she's gone to work," her dad said. "You better sit down while I tell you what's happened. Your mam will have her side, but I'm telling you mine and you can make your own mind up."

Jimmy went into the kitchen to boil the kettle, but then looking at the hammered kitchen unit, he said sheepishly, "I took out my temper on the kitchen sink last night."

Mary got up and was horrified to see the damage in the kitchen. "Dad, what happened?" she asked sadly.

"Go and sit down. I'll make the tea and I'll tell you all about it."

Jimmy turned on the charm for his gullible daughter, telling her how he loved this woman he had married in the war. How the chance meeting from the advert in the Gazette had blossomed their love once again and how he admired his old flame, Sonia, for being so determined to find him again after all these years.

Mary looked at her father, unable to see through the deceitful web of intrigue he was telling her. At the same time, she felt heartily sorry for her mother who would have put up with anything as long as he stayed with her.

She stayed until her mother was due in from work, watching and entertaining the children while her father got bathed and ready to see if he could get a flat from the council.

Jimmy managed to get out of the house before Lizzie came in from work and when she did, she brought her daughter into the kitchen so that she could tell her side of the story. Then, as if to seal the tale of her trauma, she pulled off her cardigan to reveal the horrific bruises she had suffered at the hands of her husband.

Mary stood still, unable to offer any comfort to her distant mother whose only show of genuine affection was when Mary had given birth to her grandson.

Lizzie pulled her cardigan back to cover her arms again and said, "Well, what did he have to say?"

Mary answered slowly, "He said he was going to get a flat. You know, mam, you'll be better on your own. I'll be able to help you with Deborah…"

"I know. I don't need him. He'll regret ever leaving me, I know that." Lizzie made the statement with bitter resentment as she finally accepted that it was over.

"Mam, I know a solicitor where I work," Mary said. "Come with me and talk to her. You know you have to…"

Chapter 24

Lizzie came back from her daydreaming to the sound of her mother shouting that a meal was on the table if she could eat a bite.

For a brief instant, it felt as though she was fifteen again, Mam and Dad downstairs, her sisters fighting over who got to use the kitchen sink first and that flutter of apprehension before her very first day at work.

But then she sat up from the bed and the aching of her back and knees reminded her that, no, she wasn't fifteen any longer...

She raised her eyes to the clock that was still ticking on the wall. Look at the time, she thought. She must have fallen asleep.

But more than that, a whole lifetime had passed.

The bedroom didn't smell of Mam's perfume or Alice's pan stick, it smelled musty, an old room in an old house with only memories from long ago. Memories of home and family.

Her hand brushed against the cool paper of the envelope.

Divorce papers.

Her attempts to make a family of her own were in ruins now. She sat there, looking at the envelope, wishing she had never got involved with Jimmy from Wright's biscuit factory... why could she have not settled for second best in Billy and the boring security he could have given her?

Her mind drifted back. Jimmy from Wright's biscuit factory... charming Jimmy... funny, exciting, kind Jimmy who had swept her off her feet all that time ago... her very own Gentleman Jim. How could she ever really wish it had been any different...?

She pondered over the papers, she would now be a divorced women, a lone parent with Deborah.

What would the new chapter in her life bring?